He...was...gorgeous

Not too much hair on his chest. And he had to be into lifting weights to get rounded pecs like that. Such perfection couldn't be achieved any other way.

The hard ground sloped to the edge of the river, though not as much as Karrie would've liked for privacy. Rob found a small boulder and drew her behind it, the surface hot with the desert's broiling sun.

"You gonna take that off?" Rob asked, cocking one eyebrow, indicating her T-shirt.

"Silly me." She returned his smile and pulled up the hem of her shirt, but then teasingly dropped it again.

Rob laughed. "So that's how it is." He caught her around the waist.

Giggling, Karrie twisted and wiggled, but couldn't stop him from getting hold of her top and pulling it over her head. She stumbled backward but caught her balance, still chuckling.

But Rob wasn't laughing anymore. His hungry gaze roamed her breasts, her bare midriff. By the time his eyes met hers, her nipples had tightened.

"Come here" was all he had to say....

Blaze™

Dear Reader,

Wow, has time flown by!

This is my sixth Blaze novel. Meanwhile, it feels like only last month that I first learned of the sexy, hot new series being introduced by Harlequin. It took me all of two seconds to say I wanted in. And I quickly put my imagination to work. What I've enjoyed most are the strong, confident, "bring-it-on" heroines I get to write about. In *Good To Be Bad,* which is set in my own backyard of Las Vegas, my heroine, Karrie Albright, knows what she wants—her former professor. Once she's set her sights on him, he doesn't stand a chance. Sheesh, if only I'd been that confident....

I hope you enjoy Karrie and Rob's adventure!

Best,

Debbi Rawlins

Books by Debbi Rawlins

HARLEQUIN BLAZE

*Men To Do

GOOD TO BE BAD

Debbi Rawlins

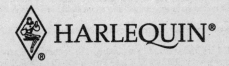

HARLEQUIN®

TORONTO • NEW YORK • LONDON
AMSTERDAM • PARIS • SYDNEY • HAMBURG
STOCKHOLM • ATHENS • TOKYO • MILAN • MADRID
PRAGUE • WARSAW • BUDAPEST • AUCKLAND

This one's for Vicky, Iona and Karl,
my inherited family and the best stepchildren
I could have. But just remember, y'all
are too old to call me Mom.

ISBN 0-373-79163-1

GOOD TO BE BAD

Copyright © 2004 by Debbi Quattrone.

www.eHarlequin.com

Printed in U.S.A.

Prologue

KARRIE ALBRIGHT LOOKED AROUND the crowded living room of the impeccably decorated SoHo brownstone and wondered again what the hell she was doing here. Another Friday night, another party with meaningless chitchat, vague passes from men who'd sell their own mothers for a decent day at the brokerage and scathing looks from women who wouldn't be caught dead in anything less than designer labels.

The saving grace was, of course, that she was here with Madison. Karrie had never quite figured out why the two of them kept getting invited to these soirees, given that neither of them were terribly hip, they preferred jeans to Dolce & Gabbana, and they weren't in the same hemisphere when it came to income, but about two years ago, they'd hooked up with marvelously witty book editor Nancy Kragen, and they'd been included ever since.

It was great to have a regular social outlet, and they'd met some terrific women and a few nice men, but lately, the parties had been, well, getting stale.

"You don't believe in this nonsense, do you?" Madison asked, her gaze focused on the door to Sonya's bedroom.

"Of course not."

The door opened and Karrie ducked to get a look at the infamous Madam Zora. Last month, one of the girls had had a candle party, the month before that, Madison's friend Elizabeth had thrown a roll-your-own-sushi night. But this had to be the weakest get-together of the year. A psychic? Please. "Are you going to sign up for a reading?"

Madison rolled her eyes. "I'm not wasting my time."

"As if you have anything better to do." Karrie cast a dismal gaze around the room. Women outnumbered the eligible men by three to one. She loved Manhattan but this was getting old. "Come on. We're here. I can't bear to go home yet. You know what night this is, right?"

"Ah, yes. The ever-popular Mr. Warzowski's night for screaming at his wife as he goes through two cases of Rolling Rock beer."

"You've gotta love three-floor walk-ups with paper-thin walls."

"That are more expensive than most five-bedroom houses in any other state."

"But at least the heat doesn't work in the winter and there's none of that noisy air-conditioning in the summer."

Madison nodded and had another big sip of martini. "Girlfriend, it's tough for us young, gorgeous career gals."

Karrie's eyebrows rose. "Gorgeous?" It was true for Madison, of course, with her willowy figure and stunning blond hair. Karrie herself never considered her own looks to be anything more than passable. Her saving grace was that she didn't have to fight the weight battle too much, and that her hair wasn't a disaster, but her mouth was too big, her eyes not big enough, and of course, being around the professionally beautiful women in New York could bruise anyone's ego.

"Hey," Madison said, "if we can't play pretend, I really am leaving."

"Which is exactly why we're going to see Madam Zora."

"Oh, no."

"Oh, yes. You and I. Together."

Madison shook her head. "I don't know what Sonya was thinking."

"Probably trying to take our mind off the fact that we have a better chance of winning the lottery than we do of getting lucky tonight." Karrie sipped her peach martini and watched a tall woman with dark waist-length hair and red lipstick emerge from the room. Her dramatically made-up eyes widened when Nancy, who looked ravishing, damn her, in a Prada wrap, asked her what happened with the psychic.

"She's amazing. Totally awesome." The woman, who'd never been to one of the regular shindigs, shook her head, her expression a haze of disbelief. "She knew everything about me. Even that I'm engaged."

Madison poked Karrie in the ribs, then nodded at the rock on the woman's finger.

Karrie hid a smile. "Come on, you chicken. What can it hurt?"

"Don't make me do this. I hate this kind of stuff. You know I break out in hives when I'm exposed to too much schlock in one evening."

Karrie laughed, but she wasn't about to ease up on her friend. "Madison, don't be such a wet blanket. Who knows, maybe she's going to see a tall, handsome stranger in your future."

"Yeah, right."

"Okay, so she won't. But do it anyway. Please?"

"Fine."

"Okay, then."

Madison caught a passing waiter and exchanged her empty glass for another martini.

"You're really not nervous about this?"

"Of course not. It's all nonsense."

Karrie grinned. "Good. Because I put our names down an hour ago. We're next."

Madison glared at her at the same time the door opened and Camilla, of candle party fame, emerged, her face flushed, the sparkle in her eyes an odd mixture of fear and excitement. Which was strange, because Camilla wasn't the type to be snowed by a con game.

Karrie suddenly had second thoughts. Maybe this wasn't such a great idea. What if Madam Zora predicted something bad about Karrie's job? Like that she wouldn't get promoted to Public Relations Director when her boss retired at the end of next year? Or that she'd lose the apartment on Sixth, even though she'd been on the waiting list for over a year.

Her thoughts suddenly turned to her brother, stationed in Germany. If Madam Zora…

No, it was all twaddle. Pure guff. Nothing but the science of watching people and playing the odds. Psychics kept things so general the facts could fit hundreds of people. Even if Madam Zora guessed Karrie had a brother, she wasn't going to know anything real about him. Now that she thought about it, she hadn't called him in too long, and that was her bad.

Regardless of psychic predictions, his job as an air force pilot wasn't without risk. Like her, he'd been desperate to leave Searchlight where they'd grown up and he'd joined the service the day he was eligible.

Karrie had used a college scholarship to escape the small desert town, and since their mother had remarried and left five years ago, neither of them had returned to Nevada, or the shabby trailer that had provided no privacy, only a lot of shame.

She swallowed and turned back to Madison, who was busy nibbling a blini with a dollop of sour cream and a smidge of caviar. "You don't think she'd predict anything bad, do you?"

Annoying amusement lifted Madison's eyebrows. "Like what?"

"I don't know. Like a death, or something."

"And ruin Sonya's party? Don't be droll." Madison frowned. "But if she says anything negative about my next photo shoot, I'll kill myself."

"Which one?"

Madison grinned slyly. "For *Today's Man.*"

"No way. Which issue?"

Her smile broadened.

Karrie stepped back. "The sexiest man layout?"

"Yep."

"Oh my God. That's terrific! When were you going to tell me?"

"I got the call this afternoon. I still can't believe it myself."

Karrie raised her glass. "Congratulations, girlfriend."

"Save the kudos until I get the man-of-the-year cover."

Karrie sighed. "Would you chill out long enough to enjoy the moment? This is major. World class. How many photographers vie for that shoot each month? And you got it."

"Yeah, but—"

"Nope." She held up a hand. "I'm not listening to any 'yeah buts.' You're too hard on yourself. You're a damn good photographer, and you deserve the assignment. Period. Which state are you covering?"

"New York. I'm shooting right here in Manhattan."

"Cool. Who's the guy?"

"I don't know for sure yet but I think—"

"Hey, Karrie, Madison." Sonya waved them toward the bedroom. "Madam Zora is waiting for you."

"Great," Madison muttered as she finished off her drink.

Chuckling, Karrie led the way, although she wasn't quite as enthusiastic about the reading as she had been a few minutes ago. Her heart started to race as soon as she stepped into the dimly lit room. Sonya had put up some curtains to hide her bed, and made the area for the reading intimate and exotic, especially given that the only light came from the soft glow of twin candles. At the far end of the room sat Madam Zora. She wasn't quite the perfect stereotype of a parlor psychic, but she came close.

Her eyes and short hair were so black that she seemed to blend into the draped walls. Even the caftan she wore was black but still couldn't hide her large, languorous form as she lounged on a burgundy velvet love seat. Giant gold hoops glinted from her ears, tugging at the misshapen lobes with their weight.

Behind them, Sonya closed the door making Karrie jump.

"Do not be nervous, child. Come. Sit." Madam Zora motioned them to the two chairs opposite her, her smile displaying the flash of a gold tooth.

Karrie sat first, and then gave Madison the eye when it looked as if her friend might bolt.

Madison didn't even try to hide her reluctance as she finally sank into the other chair. She slid Karrie a look of barely disguised repugnance.

Madam Zora laughed softly. Hard to tell her age. Her

skin was smooth but she had old eyes. Kind eyes that immediately put Karrie at ease.

"Tell me why you've come to see Madam Zora," the woman said, looking at Karrie.

She shrugged, and said bluntly, "This isn't something I'd normally do. I don't really believe in this stuff, but I figured that since you're here and I'm not paying for it…"

Madam Zora laughed again. It was a surprisingly soothing sound. "You needn't fear me. You have a very bright future." She leaned forward and reached for Karrie's hand.

Karrie jumped just a little at the first touch, but Madam Zora's fingers calmed her as no words could.

"Work is going well for you," the psychic said with her low, slightly accented voice. "A promotion is in your future. I see—" She stopped, briefly closing her eyes.

Karrie slid a peek at Madison, who still looked as if she was at a tent revival and Madam Zora was the snake.

"B.A." Madam Zora's lids lifted. "You know someone with these initials, yes?"

Karrie nodded slowly.

"Brian?"

"Yes." Her heart somersaulted. How could this woman know her brother's name? Sonya couldn't have told her. She didn't know. "What about him?"

Madam Zora squeezed her hand. "Not to worry. He's fine, and happy to soar like a bird."

Karrie coughed, her gaze flying to her friend. Madison knew Brian was a pilot and she looked a little taken aback, too.

"Why do you bring him up?" Karrie asked.

"He is someone close to you and he's on your mind." She shrugged her thick shoulders. "Just as your job is." She stopped, frowning. "Who is R.P.? Your boyfriend?"

Karrie shook her head. "Me? Boyfriend? Uh, no." Madam Zora looked surprised, and then she closed her eyes. "You know this man. From long ago. But you will soon cross paths again."

Not likely. Karrie sighed. She rarely met eligible men in Manhattan, much less someone from her past.

Madam Zora, her eyes still closed, started fanning herself. Perspiration beaded above her upper lip. Yet it wasn't hot. In fact, cool April air slipped in through an open window.

"Oh, my, child. It will be hot when you meet again. Very hot. But you are used to the desert heat, yes?" Her eyes opened, her gaze spearing Karrie with a knowing look.

She straightened. This was very bizarre. Someone had to have told the woman Karrie was from Nevada. She rubbed a palm over her jeans, suddenly feeling too warm in her blazer. The thing was, she had no intention of ever returning to the Southwest.

At least the spell had been broken, and she could see the psychic for the fraud she was.

Karrie forced a polite smile, wishing the woman would turn her attention to Madison.

No such luck. If anything, Madam Zora's interest intensified. After staring at Karrie for another minute, she closed her eyes, amusement lifting her lips as if enjoying a scene playing out in her head.

"What?" Karrie asked in spite of herself.

The woman took her time, making Karrie squirm. When she finally opened her eyes, her wary look had Karrie swallowing hard.

"It will not be an ordinary affair you will be having with this man."

Madison chuckled and Karrie fought the urge to laugh herself. Madam Zora was so off base. Going back to the desert to have a hot and heavy affair? She thought of her work calendar and how booked she was clear into next year. Not a chance in hell.

"No, my dear. It's not a joke. I see this quite clearly. Your relationship will be very physical at first," the psychic continued, her eyes sparkling. "Very sexual, very raw. Primitive," she whispered in a husky voice.

Karrie shivered and her smile died on her lips. Something about the woman's voice, the way dark eyes flashed made her words almost plausible.

"You won't be able to keep your hands off each other, even though you will both try hard to stay apart. But the chemistry between you won't allow it. Even the desert heat will not diminish your passion."

"I'm sorry," Karrie said, ready to turn the focus of

the session to her friend. "This is all very fanciful, but there's definitely no desert heat in my future."

"So you believe today."

"I do."

Madam Zora's smile made Karrie's heart beat a little faster. "It will happen sooner than you could possibly know. You will go back to the desert. You will meet this man once more. And you will try very hard to disbelieve your heart."

"My heart?"

"That, my dear girl, will be the only thing you can truly count on. Remember these words."

"I will."

Madam Zora chuckled softly. "Yes, I know. Although you'll try to deny it, but there are strong forces at work here."

Karrie nodded as if she were serious, then decided to move things along. "I don't mean to change the subject, but do you happen to see anything in my future about a new apartment?" Not that she'd believe her.

The psychic sighed, shook her head, making the gold hoops dance in the candlelight. "I'm sorry, there will be no new apartment."

Karrie glanced quickly at Madison, then her gaze went back to the charlatan in front of her. "No?"

"But it will not matter."

"Okay then," Karrie said. "Thank you for the wonderful session. I know Madison is anxious to hear what you see in her future."

Madison made a small choking sound, but Karrie paid it no heed. She'd had enough, and all she wanted now was to have another martini and see if there were any of those hors d'oeuvres left.

1

"YOU ASKED TO SEE ME?" Karrie stood tentatively at Malcolm Sandhill's office door, waiting for him to look up at her with his ridiculously bushy graying eyebrows.

He frowned briefly at her before returning to leaf through the stack of papers in front of him. "Karrie Albright, from our PR department, right?"

"Yes," she murmured, annoyed that the vice president of operations didn't recognize her immediately. Although he really shouldn't. After all, she was still a peon at Sanax, even though she'd been working there for two years. But the multinational corporation was so huge, and had its finger in so many pies, it was easy to get lost. At least after her boss retired next year and she became manager of the PR department, she'd be one more big rung up the ladder.

"Come in, Ms. Albright. Sit down." He barely looked up from the piece of paper he studied.

She walked into the room, her gaze immediately drawn to the expansive windows and the awesome view of Central Park. She'd never so much as peeked into the plush corner office before, and she certainly hadn't been summoned by Mr. Sandhill before today.

A little nervous, she sat on the edge of the brown leather chair and waited for him to say something. There was a scent to the room, despite its size and the immaculate neatness. It reminded her of her favorite bookstore where she often had coffee and read for hours on her days off.

The sound of papers shuffling brought her attention back to the senior vice president across the desk. His gaze narrowed on what she recognized as a company memo and she wondered why his wife didn't get him to trim his eyebrows. "I understand you're from Nevada. A town called Searchlight."

Not something she necessarily liked to think about, but slowly she nodded, her curiosity skyrocketing.

"Our Nevada office has received a request from the University of Nevada Las Vegas to use some Sanax land located about two hours outside of the city near a place called Laughlin. Are you familiar with that area?"

"Yes, sir."

"Good." He slid the memo across the desk toward her. "The archeology department wants to establish a dig on our property, and I want to examine the ramifications. I want all the specs on the land—possible uses, value, demographics. Make certain that if anything of significance is uncovered, it won't hamper any potential revenue."

It took her a moment to wrap her head around the direction of the conversation. It was so out of left field, but she wasn't about to show Sandhill she wasn't quick on the uptake. "I assume the dig is focusing on Paiute artifacts?"

She caught a hint of a smile, which disappeared so fast she might have imagined it. "That's correct."

"I see." Her thoughts turned to her days at the University of Nevada Las Vegas. She'd majored in business but studied archeology for one semester during her junior year because of the hunky teacher.

Although it had been five years since she graduated, she wasn't likely to forget Dr. Philips...try as she might. She'd made such an ass out of herself. But so did half the other girls in his class, which had been predominately female. He hadn't so much as flinched at any of the attention. The general consensus was that he had to be gay.

"Ms. Albright?" The sharpness in Sandhill's tone startled her and she realized she'd drifted.

"I was just wondering," she said quickly, "what makes them think there are any artifacts of significance left? The area has been pretty well scoured in the past few decades."

"They admit as much but apparently it's the digging experience they want for the students. Be that as it may, I don't want them finding anything that would preclude us from using the land."

"Which is slated for...?"

This time he did smile, albeit briefly. "Nothing at the moment. I assume you know the history of the corporation?"

Karrie nodded. She'd written tomes on the very subject. Sanax was bought from the heirs of a private owner about seven years ago, and had gone public under the new management. The previous owner had had more money than financial sense. He'd used company profits to buy up all kinds of land on speculation. A small percentage of it had paid off but the rest was just sitting there while branch managers all over the world investigated the profit potential. "So this land is still in limbo."

"That's correct, although the preliminary findings haven't been encouraging. It is in the middle of the desert."

"So was Laughlin once," she said.

"Which is one of the reasons I want this land assessed."

Her gaze strayed out the window as she enjoyed a brief daydream about having her own corner office with this awesome view. If she played her cards right, this could be her chance to shine. She looked back at him and found annoyance in his eyes. "I have a few questions," she said. "First, may I ask why the Nevada office isn't handling this?"

"I have them busy on another matter."

"Fine," she said, knowing from his tone that the subject was closed. "My understanding is that the office there is having problems with Clark County over water rights."

He nodded, frowning. "Very touchy."

"If we do decide to let the University have their dig, we could parlay that into an excellent PR opportunity. If played well, those water-rights issues may take a sudden turn."

Sandhill's eyes lit up. "I can see that we made a wise choice having you head up the project. Look into it and report back directly to me."

"Yes, sir." She rose when she realized his attention had already shifted to something else on his desk.

"Ms. Albright?"

She paused halfway to the door and looked at him. It dawned on her that his perpetual frown didn't mean he was unhappy, just that he was deep in thought. She filed that tidbit away for further study.

"My secretary will make your travel arrangements. Tell her you'll be leaving tomorrow."

Karrie lost the smile. "Pardon me, sir, you want me to physically go to Las Vegas?"

This time his frown wasn't pensive. "Is that a problem?"

"I believe I can handle the entire investigation from here. I'll simply coordinate with the Nevada branch, and have the report for you in—"

Impatience drew his bushy eyebrows together.

"Sir, I'm in the middle of a project for the Macy's Thanksgiving Day parade and—"

"That can wait," Sandhill said. "This matter can't. We have to get back to the University with our answer as soon as possible."

She took a deep breath and swallowed several arguments that were on the tip of her tongue.

"Ms. Albright, I'm giving you the chance to put your best foot forward. If we do support the dig, I don't simply want a press release. I want you in front of the news cameras extolling our generosity."

"Ah, I see, sir." God, she did not want to go back to Las Vegas. Not even for a single day. "And I do appreciate the opportunity."

"I'll expect to hear from you next week. In the meantime, show the community we at Sanax are team players."

She barely held her tongue at his flip use of *we*. "I'll update my supervisor and plan on leaving tomorrow."

By way of dismissal, he picked up a file folder and opened it. "Gerda will let our people in Vegas know you're going out there."

A funny feeling niggled at her. "Who's my contact at the University?"

He didn't look up but glanced at the memo. "Dr. Philips. Dr. Rob Philips."

R.P.

Karrie couldn't move. She simply stared at the top of Sandhill's graying head, her stomach doing flip-flops as the words of Madam Zora came back to haunt her.

ROB GOT OUT OF HIS CAR and looked down at his shoes. Great time to check and see if they matched. The Sanax representative was to meet him in five minutes. He hoped she wasn't late. A dozen midterm exams waited grading in his office.

He hated this part of his job. Having to schmooze with corporations for either endowments or land use. The only thing worse was dealing with academic bureaucracy. But he played the games so that he could have freedom in the field. He'd learned the hard way to carefully choose his battles.

Having been a child prodigy had its drawbacks. He'd entered college too young, graduated too young and earned his Ph.D. at the age most people were figuring out their majors. Along the way social and tactical skills had lagged. He'd had his share of butting heads with the Dean and board members because he lacked the diplomacy and the patience that presumably came with age.

He wove through the parking lot of Joe's Crab Shack, thinking again how peculiar it was that the rep had requested they meet at a restaurant. Probably figured he owed her dinner after having to come all the way from New York. Little did she know he'd do a lot more than spring for a meal to gain access to this particular site. Hell, he'd get down on his hands and knees and suck up big time if he had to.

Already having forgotten her name, he patted his pocket for the piece of paper the department secretary had given him. But, because he'd done something vile in a past life, it wasn't there. He was cursed with a total lack of memory when it came to names. Modern ones, that is. He could list all the Greek gods from Atlas to Zeus without blinking. But anyone from this lifetime, and he was hopeless. It didn't seem to matter that he'd repeated the name of the cursed woman over and over before leaving for the restaurant. All he could remember were initials. K.A.

He got inside the cool restaurant, and despite his fervent wishes the hostess informed him the Sanax watchdog hadn't arrived yet, so he followed dutifully to their reserved table and ordered a glass of wine while he waited.

The place was starting to fill up and he hoped he wouldn't see any of his students. Even though he didn't get out much he seemed to run into someone from one of his classes every place he went. Which was one reason he didn't circulate often. Young women appeared to be getting increasingly bold each year.

Although the restaurant area wasn't too crowded yet, the bar was lined with happy-hour patrons, some of them standing for lack of stools. His gaze immediately was drawn to a redhead sitting at the end of the bar. Really more auburn, her curly hair was tied at her nape and hung halfway down her back.

Even in a khaki skirt she had a great backside, curvy and lush just as it should be. What he could see of her legs made his pulse quicken. Slender yet rounded with just the right amount of muscle.

A man walked up and said something to her and

when she turned her head to respond, Rob thought there was something vaguely familiar about her. The slightly upturned nose, high cheekbones, the long graceful neck… She wasn't one of his students. He was sure he'd remember. Even in his Thursday lectures where attendance often reached a hundred and fifty she would've stood out.

Anyway, she was too old to be a student. Probably in her mid to late twenties. Which automatically didn't rule out the possibility except she was dressed in business attire. So where the hell could he have seen her before?

"Here you go." The waitress set down his wine and smiled. "Did you want to order, or are you still waiting on someone?"

"Still waiting, thanks."

"How about an appetizer in the meantime? The crab and artichoke dip is excellent. We also have an assorted shrimp platter."

"No, thanks anyway." What he wanted was for her to move and not block his view of the bar.

"Okay, I'll check back later."

As soon as she stepped away his gaze returned to the woman sitting at the bar. She was gone. The bartender cleared her empty glass and another woman claimed the chair.

Rob glanced around but didn't see the redhead. She'd probably left with the guy who'd been talking to her. It didn't matter. It wasn't as if Rob would've tried to pick her up. That wasn't his style.

Nevertheless, he took another cursory glance around the room and came up empty. He checked his watch. She was one minute late. He muttered a curse as he reached into his pocket to check once again for the slip of paper with her name on it. He was supposed to be a bright guy with a high IQ. One would think he could remember a name for more than three minutes.

K.A. It should have been enough of a reminder to give him the whole name, but it didn't. He had no clue.

Taking a sip of his wine, he glanced in the direction of the hostess stand. Two couples hovered, waiting for her attention. Rob rolled a shoulder, curious at the tension cramping his muscles and making him inexplicably edgy.

This meeting wasn't going to be a big deal. Just a formality. He didn't expect them to turn down his request. They'd already given every indication that there'd be no problem with the dig. Although why they didn't simply send him approval in writing he didn't understand.

Maybe it was his guilty conscience making him uneasy. He hadn't been totally forthcoming about his reason for selecting that particular site. Still, it shouldn't matter to Sanax. The land was virtually useless. At least to them.

He took another sip of wine, and as he set down the glass, he saw her. The redhead was coming from the other side of the restaurant. He tried not to stare but the snug fit of her blouse and the way her breasts jiggled slightly reduced his resolve. She had a small waist, too, with a nice flare to her hips. Nothing emaciated or boy-ish about her.

As she got closer he forced himself to look away, hoping his appointment showed up before he got stu-pid enough to ask the redhead to have a drink.

"Dr. Philips?"

He turned. She stood in front of him, a tentative smile curving her lips. "Yes," he said slowly, pleased yet disappointed that she obviously knew him. He'd really hate if she turned out to be a student, after all. But now that she was up close, she really looked familiar.

Her smile faltered. "You probably don't remember me."

Frowning, he studied her more closely, and when her tongue slipped out to touch the corner of her mouth, recognition instantly dawned. "Karrie?"

Slowly she nodded.

That name he hadn't forgotten. What amazed him was how he could have forgotten that face for a single instant. She'd been the one student, the only one, who'd nearly been his undoing. He struggled for composure. "It's been a long time. Five, six years?"

"Something like that." She pulled out a chair and sat down. "How have you been?"

He glanced over his shoulder, surprised at her push-iness in inviting herself to his table. He remembered her as being a little on the shy side. Certainly not like some of the other more brazen female students.

Not that he didn't want to talk with her, catch up on what she'd been doing, but he still had to meet with the Sanax watchdog. Besides, just seeing her again had knocked the wind out of him, and he needed to be on his toes. She wasn't his student anymore. No more boundaries. And he was definitely interested. But first, business.

"Dr. Philips? Is anything wrong?"

He met her puzzled eyes. Hazel. More golden than green. And lashes that were naturally long and thick. He'd never been this close to her before. He'd made it a point not to.

"No, not exactly. I, um…"

She sucked in her lower lip, making the tiny dimple at one corner of her mouth more pronounced. It looked as if she'd pulled her hair back tighter since she'd been sitting at the bar, but escaped tendrils curled around her face, a mass of golden highlights picked up by the flickering light from the candle on the table.

"Good evening. May I get you something to drink?" The waitress said, making him jump. He hadn't even seen her approach. "A glass of wine while you look at the menu maybe?"

"Just some iced tea, please." Karrie smiled at the other woman and then looked back at him. "I got here early and had something at the bar already."

Damn. How was he going to do this tactfully?

"Look, Karrie," he said as soon as the waitress left. "I'd really like to hear about what you've been doing. Maybe you could give me your number and—"

She looked affronted.

This was precisely the type of situation he tried to avoid. Small talk, especially with women, was not his strong suit. He always managed to say the wrong thing. "The truth is, I'm here to meet someone. It's business."

Her confused frown deepened, her lush full lips parting provocatively. It threw him off balance and he fumbled for the right words that wouldn't sound as if he were blowing her off.

He pushed a hand through his hair, then checked his watch. "Do you have plans later?"

Her eyebrows rose. "I don't think so."

"This meeting I have. It shouldn't take long." He gave her one of those grins his secretary described as devilishly boyish and shrugged. "I'm trying to sweet-talk some corporation rep into letting me use the company's land for a dig. I don't think it's going to be a problem. Probably just want to make me jump through a few hoops before they agree."

Her eyes briefly widened and then a smile tugged at the corners of her mouth. "Well, start jumping and sweet-talking. I'm the Sanax rep."

2

ROB STARED AT HER, hoping like hell she was kidding. Finally, he laughed. "You have a wicked sense of humor."

She pressed her lips together, looking entirely too serious. "I really am from Sanax."

"You're here from New York?"

Lifting a shoulder, she nodded.

"Damn."

She smiled again. "It's not as if you said anything bad. I mean, you could've described how you were gonna suck up to me and all that. Which I would've enjoyed, actually."

He grunted.

Karrie laughed. "Okay, I should have introduced myself right away, but I figured since you had my name and knew who I was…"

The name hadn't registered. Even after he recognized her. Karrie, herself, was another story. That hair, those lips… He cleared his throat. "Sorry. I hope you didn't think I was hitting on you."

"I'm flattered."

At a loss for words, he studied her for a moment. She'd changed. She seemed more sophisticated. More confident. Not that he'd ever really known her, but there was something about the way she looked him directly in the eyes…

"Okay," he said, anxious to get back to business, an area in which he was more comfortable. "Do you want to talk about the site or should we order dinner first?"

"Dinner. I haven't eaten since I left New York this morning." She picked up the menu and peered down at it, while nibbling at her lower lip.

Instead of perusing his own menu, he watched her study the list of items with the concentration of a student preparing for a quiz. The thought occurred to him that gaining access to the land might not be as easy as he'd thought. Dealing with someone from the urban East wasn't the same as trying to sidestep a local.

Most people from around here were too familiar with the odd discovery of a vein of silver or finds of an important historic burial ground. Sanax wouldn't want the land tampered with, unless it was by their own people who could swiftly take advantage of any discovery.

Karrie had probably only come to Las Vegas for college, like most of the student body. And like the rest of the kids, her agenda had been grades and dates, not local environmental and cultural issues. He hoped so, anyway.

"Any recommendations?" she asked, and looked up to catch him staring.

He quickly turned his attention to the menu. "Uh,

yeah. The coconut shrimp is good, and so are the bacon-wrapped scallops."

"Ever have the seafood bisque?"

"Many times. The chowder isn't bad, either."

"Sounds like you eat here often."

"The Crab Shack on the other side of town, but yeah, probably too often."

"I guess that means no wife and kids at home." She moistened her lips, the action threatening his resolve to stay on the business track.

"Nope. What about you?"

She gave a startled laugh. "I'm too young to be tied down."

"I hear you."

She frowned. "Can I ask you something personal?"

"Go ahead." He didn't promise to answer, although he had a feeling he knew what the question was.

"How old are you?"

He smiled. "Too young to have been a professor when I had you as a student."

"Seriously, you didn't look much older than we did."

"I'm thirty-one. You were in my class—when? five years ago?"

"Six."

"Ah. You were the first class I taught after getting my Ph.D. I'd just turned twenty-five that spring."

Her eyebrows rose. "You had to have entered college at a really young age."

"Sixteen."

"That must have been tough."

He shrugged. "Not academically, but I definitely was socially challenged."

She wrinkled her nose, and damn if even that didn't make her look sexy. "I have another question for you."

"Shoot."

"Did you know that the entire female portion of your class had the hots for you?"

Embarrassed, taken by surprise, Rob half grunted, half laughed. "Students were and still are off limits."

"Which doesn't answer my question."

"Yeah, I knew."

"I see."

He tilted his head slightly to the right, looking at her with teasing eyes. "You were one of those females."

Color climbed her cheeks, and she picked up her iced tea. "I was only twenty," she murmured.

"Now it's my turn to be flattered."

She started laughing midsip and quickly lowered the glass and licked the splattered moisture from her lips. "I deserved that."

"No comment."

"Good move."

He smiled. Neither diplomacy nor chivalry had shut him up. He was too busy watching her tongue sweep her lower lip to think of anything clever to say. And how that tiny dimple flashed at the corner of her mouth, calling further attention to that wide sexy mouth of hers.

Their eyes met. Neither of them spoke.

For an instant he recalled the first time he'd seen her in one of his lectures, sitting midway up the stadium-style seating. There had to have been at least a hundred students, but the light shining on her wild auburn hair had caught his eye. She'd given him a shy smile that forced his gaze down to his notes for the next forty minutes.

"You folks ready to order?"

Karrie blinked at the waitress as if she had no idea what the woman was talking about.

Before Rob could rebound and respond, the waitress said, "Maybe I should give you a few more minutes."

"Great," Karrie said at the same time Rob said, "We're ready."

The waitress smiled. "I'll be back in a few."

"I'll just order a salad," Karrie murmured and closed her menu. "I know you're anxious to get this meeting over with."

"No, please, take your time."

She set the menu aside, braced her arms on the table and leaned forward. "You're right. We don't object to your dig, and it's entirely reasonable to assume that by tomorrow afternoon I'll be getting back to you with written consent. Tomorrow morning I have to check with county records. My plane was delayed or I would have already done that."

"What are you looking for at county records?" He didn't like the way she was all business suddenly.

Her gaze narrowed slightly. "Do you expect to find anything?"

"No." He shrugged. "I mean I hope the kids find a few arrowheads and maybe some broken pottery. Just to keep the dig interesting. But generally I just want them to go through the paces."

She nodded. "So we should have no problem."

"None." Shit, he hoped not. As far as he knew, his friend Joe Tonopah was the only one who believed there might be a Paiute burial ground in the area. "What's Sanax planning on doing with the land?"

"Nothing, so far. It was bought on speculation a long time ago. Personally, I think it'll end up being a zero for us."

Good. He didn't have to feel too bad about not being totally honest with her. His friend Joe was eighty-eight and the diabetes had taken its toll. Rob had made him a promise he intended to keep. Even if it meant deceiving Karrie.

THE WAITRESS RETURNED, and after they'd ordered and she left, an awkward silence stretched. Damn, Karrie wished she'd never met Madam Zora. Bad enough her nerves were shot to hell just sitting across from him, but every time her mind wandered back to what the psychic had predicted two months ago, she'd get all jittery inside.

Hard to come across mature and sophisticated when her palms were so clammy that she avoided picking up her glass. It didn't matter. She wasn't his student anymore, and he wasn't married. If he was attached, he'd have to speak up. Because as soon as business was out of the way, she was going for it.

Talk about the perfect Man To Do. He fit the bill in every way. She'd had such an incredible crush on him all those years ago. In fact, that crush had actually hampered her social life. None of the boys at school could compete with the handsome professor. He'd been such a fascinating bundle of contradictions. He knew his material extraordinarily well, and taught with a passion that had fascinated her with a subject that had never made her pause. And yet there was a shy quality that showed up the second he wasn't talking about the land, or the artifacts. He'd blushed back then, and every time he did, half the women in the class swooned. It was just so charming.

Everything had gotten worse when she'd gone on her first dig with him. Because that's when she'd seen him without his shirt. Oh, mama, that wasn't something she'd ever forget. Sculpted like a masterwork, tan, muscled so perfectly it was more than human, it was art.

If she'd dreamed about him once, she'd dreamed about him a hundred times. Every one of those dreams had ended with them making love. Of course, he'd made it perfectly clear that she was a student and only that back then. But now?

She could see he was interested. She wasn't leaving until tomorrow night. Which left a tantalizing window of opportunity, and what was the Man To Do about if not seizing the day?

She'd been in the e-mail group for a little over a year, enjoying the frank discussions with incredibly bright and witty women from all walks of life. Their most daring project was the Man To Do. The whole concept was wild and wicked. Find a guy who didn't fit into the lifetime plan, who wasn't someone to take home to Mom. Have a night, a weekend, whatever, that was purely for pleasure. For getting one's ya-yas out. Only, there hadn't been one man in New York who'd piqued her interest. Not enough to actually do the deed.

Despite the image of the *Sex and the City* and all that, she wasn't a one-night-stand kind of gal. She'd always had to have some kind of emotion attached to sex, or she wasn't interested. Not necessarily love, but something more than lust.

Rob Philips fit the bill to a T. It felt as if she'd wanted him forever, and here he was, practically served up on a silver platter.

God, she hoped the rumors that he was gay weren't true. She didn't think so. Not with the scorching way he'd been looking at her. Another reason she could barely think straight. He still had the most amazing brown eyes she'd ever seen.

Surprisingly, he looked even better than she remembered. And she'd remembered the details for far too long. The boyish grin was the same, kind of reticent and shy, but his face was more weathered. Not just tanned but more chiseled. As if he'd cosmetically added the lines fanning out at the corners of his eyes, and the small scar at his jaw had been strategically placed just so.

Hell, he'd be a perfect candidate for one of Madison's photo shoots. He had just the right look. Rugged, sexy, his intelligence shining in those remarkable eyes. Her gaze went back to that perfect little scar on his chin. Just the touch to make him seem mysterious and a wee bit dangerous. "What happened?" she asked, pointing to the mirrored spot on her own chin.

His fingers automatically went to the scarred skin. Even his hands were tan. "Rock climbing."

Not the outdoor type, she mentally shuddered. "You're lucky that's the only memento."

His mouth twisted in a wry grin. "Not exactly." He leaned back and briefly lifted his shirt to expose a nasty gash under his rib cage.

Karrie swallowed hard. Yeah, the scar was ugly and barely healed, but that wasn't what had her trying to catch her breath. The chest of her dreams had become even more enticing. He had a set of abs on him that sent an arrow of heat straight to the juncture of her thighs. "Ouch," she said finally. "When did that happen?"

"About two months ago."

"Around here?"

He gave her a sheepish look. "Yeah."

"Come on, there's a story here."

"I don't want to ruin my macho image."

She laughed. "You have to tell me now."

"I should've ordered an appetizer."

"You'd have to stop chewing eventually."

His slow grin made her feel like a silly schoolgirl again, giddy and, astonishingly, a little light-headed. This whole thing was so unreal. He wasn't just sexy but he actually had a personality. In class the only thing she'd known for sure was that he loved his career. Now she saw there was more to him than digging shards.

"You were climbing at Red Rock, right? What's the name of that place where beginners go in the Calico Basin area? I think it's called Caustic?"

He winced.

She grinned. "Am I right?"

"How do you know about Caustic? You're gonna make me look like a real wimp and tell me you climb, right?"

"God, no. Stairs. That's my limit. Quit changing the subject."

"Seriously, how do you know about Caustic?"

"I lived here, remember?"

"How long did you stay after college?"

"About a minute."

He chuckled. "You liked it here that much, eh?"

"I'm from Searchlight. Enough said."

He reared his head back. The look on his face went beyond surprise. He seemed displeased, which didn't make sense. "Searchlight?"

"I take it you've been there."

"Sure. It's small."

She smiled. "That was very diplomatic. Now, get back to the rock-climbing incident."

"You're ruthless."

"Yes, I am."

"Okay…" He rubbed his jaw near the tiny scar, looking distracted suddenly. "There's this place in Henderson where you learn to climb. Indoors, simulated. You getting the picture?"

Karrie tried not to laugh, but she couldn't help herself, which brought the smile back to his lips. "I'm impressed that you even made the attempt."

"A group of fourteen-year-olds weren't so impressed. They laughed their asses off because they had to help the old geezer down the last ten feet."

"But you were really hurt."

"They didn't know that at the time." He studied her for a moment, his eyebrows coming together in a slight frown. "You look different."

Slowly shaking her head, she shrugged. "Probably pale. We had a bad winter. Not much sun."

"It's your hair."

"Oh." She smoothed back the unruly curls. She'd left New York with a French braid, but that had been hours and two time zones ago. The best she'd been able to do on the taxi ride over was to brush it out and tie it back. "Are you saying different bad, or different good?"

His eyes crinkled at the corners. "Very good, indeed."

She felt the compliment to the tips of her toes, and her water glass held sudden interest. "Thanks," she murmured. "I like your hair, too. It's longer."

"Yeah." He looked embarrassed at the return volley. "I'd like to say I abandoned the geek look, but I just keep forgetting to get it cut."

"A geek? You?"

He picked up his glass of wine and took a sip, but not before she saw the smile tugging at the corners of his mouth. She had the feeling that if there'd ever been anything geeky about him it was because that's the way he wanted to appear.

They weren't so different. He'd embarked on his career at a young age and probably created a facade to support his image. She'd done the same after arriving in Manhattan. Convinced that she'd been the biggest hick to set foot in the city, she quickly devoured fashion magazines and spent money she could ill afford on clothes and hair care. She'd even skipped meals so that she could eat skimpy, pricey appetizers and sip expensive wine in the In restaurants.

Foolish and shallow maybe, but she didn't regret any of it. She had a great job, a terrific salary and unlimited potential if she continued to play the game. Which reminded her of the reason for being here.

"There's something else I want to go over with you," she said, at the same time she caught their waitress's eye and motioned the woman over. "I'm working on a press release about the dig."

"Pardon?"

The waitress showed up before Karrie could respond. She ordered a glass of wine for herself and another for him. He looked annoyed, but she couldn't tell if it was over the press release or her assertiveness. Probably both.

The waitress had barely taken a step toward the bar when he asked, "What about this press release?"

"No big deal." She hadn't considered how honest to be with him. "Like any large corporation we've had a few go-rounds with the County and I'm looking to get some good press out of this."

"This was your idea?"

She nodded. "I am in the PR department."

"I don't understand. Other than the press aspect, why are you involved?"

"The vice president in charge found out I knew the area and figured I might have some valuable insight. Which we both know means nothing. But I wasn't about to turn down the opportunity to strut my stuff."

He sat back, his shoulders tensing, and showed excessive interest in the antics of two teenagers who had just joined their parents at a nearby table.

She waited for him to respond but he seemed willing to let the subject drop. "Do you have a problem dealing with me?"

He sent her a quick frown. "No. Why should I?"

"You seem agitated."

The slow lazy smile was instantly back. "Actually, I'm going to enjoy working with you."

Karrie didn't quite believe it. Something had gotten him riled, but it was hard to think about much more than the way one side of his mouth always hiked up a tad before he actually smiled, or the way crisp dark hair curled at the open neck of his shirt.

She grabbed her glass of iced tea, mostly watered down but there was still some ice left, and enjoyed the cool moisture against her palm. Time to change the subject, get him back to his earlier calm. "Good God, I don't remember it being so hot this early in June." She fisted her hair, lifted it off her neck, and then with her moistened hand cupped the heated skin at her nape.

His gaze went to her throat, traveled to her scoop neckline, flickered lower for a moment before he met her eyes. "It's really not that hot yet. Besides, it's air-conditioned in here."

"Yeah, but the patio doors are open," she murmured, feeling a whole new wave of heat flushing her skin.

"Wait until late July and August."

"Thankfully, I won't be here."

He studied her thoughtfully for a moment. "Have you been back since college?"

"Once."

"To visit family?"

"Yeah, but they're gone now, too. My brother is in Germany and my mom remarried."

"So you have no reason to come back."

"None. I like my life in New York."

"Even during the winter?"

"Especially during the summer."

He smiled. "Have you noticed many changes yet?"

"Traffic is horrible."

"That's an understatement. Where are you staying?"

"The Hilton."

"The Flamingo Hilton?"

"No, I wanted to stay off the strip. In fact, if I'd made the reservation myself I would have stayed farther out."

"This place has grown so much, any farther out would have to be Searchlight."

"Funny."

"You think I'm kidding?"

She took another sip of wine, thinking back on the harrowing taxi ride from the airport. The area had really grown in the five short years since she'd been back. An entire beltway had sprung up. She couldn't help but wonder how or if Searchlight had been affected by this population explosion.

Were the trailers still there? Or had houses replaced them? Maybe there was even a high school there now, instead of the kids having to be bused over to Boulder City. Not that she was curious enough to make the fifty-mile trip to see for herself.

A wave of nostalgia took her by surprise. For years she hadn't thought about the converted carport where her mother had supported them by cutting and perming the hair of half the women in Searchlight. Or the combination drugstore-diner-gas station where Karrie used to bag Mr. Donner's trash every day to earn vanilla-and-chocolate-swirl ice-cream cones. Yet the images were all crystal clear.

The waitress brought their food and Rob immediately dug into his seafood lasagna. Not as hungry as she thought she was, Karrie eyed her shrimp and fettuccine with less enthusiasm than when she'd ordered it.

"Hey."

She looked up at him.

"Something wrong with your dinner?"

"No." She picked up a fork, not wanting to examine her sudden melancholy.

He hesitated, and then said, "Weird coming home again, huh?"

"Not really. All these people moving here." She shook her head. "I totally don't get it."

"They come for the bright lights and excitement." His teasing grin lifted her spirits and tightened her tummy.

"We have that and much more in Manhattan."

"Have you seen some of the new resorts on the strip?" he asked, keeping her gaze locked to his.

"You offering a tour?"

"Yeah."

She took a big bite of shrimp pasta. There was time enough tomorrow to talk about land and digs and Sanax. Tonight was hers, and she intended to use it in the best way possible. "I'm game," she said, hoping like hell he understood that she wasn't talking about a tour.

3

"I FEEL LIKE I'M AT A REAL BEACH instead of at a casino."

"That's the idea." Rob smiled at the look of amazement on Karrie's face as she watched the electronically generated waves crash to shore. The beach at Mandalay even had lifeguards on duty. The mega resort was one of the newer kids on the block, vying for business by making Las Vegas a family destination.

"Okay, I'm totally impressed." She turned to look at him suddenly, her hazel eyes sparkling and golden, and he had the dangerous urge to haul her against him and kiss that wide lush mouth.

"You're easy."

"Hey, don't get personal."

Hell, pretty, great legs and a sense of humor. "Wait until you see the Shark Reef."

"Would it still be open?" she asked, glancing at her watch and trying to stifle a yawn.

"I forgot you're still on East Coast time."

"No problem. I'm not ready to go to bed yet."

It was an innocuous remark. Certainly not one that could conjure such an erotic scene in his head. Karrie, sprawled out on his bed, naked, her back arching off the mattress, her golden red hair spread out like wildfire.

He shoved away from the railing they looked over. "Why don't I take you back to your hotel?"

"I have a better idea." She turned to face him, light coming from behind him glistening off her glossy pink lips. "Why don't I buy you a drink as thanks for showing me around tonight?"

"You don't have to do that."

"I know."

"Do you realize it's after midnight your time?"

"I'm a pretty bright girl. I figured that out all by myself."

"I don't remember you being such a smart-ass."

She laughed. "I'm surprised you remember me at all. You acted like you had on invisible blinders. Your attention went from the blackboard to the back of the room and didn't stop anywhere in between unless someone raised their hand."

"Right."

"It's true. Did you know we all suspected that you were gay?"

"We?"

"Some of the girls in the class."

He hadn't heard that one. "I'm not."

"I know." She turned away with a smug smile. And then frowned down at her feet. "I have got to get out of these heels."

Was that a hint? It took that little to send him back

to his earlier daydream. Even if she offered, he'd be a fool to entertain the idea of sleeping with her. Not until they made a deal about the dig. Although the ethics of the situation weren't as black-and-white as getting involved with a student, it still wasn't clear to him what kind of business relationship he and Karrie would have.

If it was true that Sanax was simply making sure they didn't waste a public relations opportunity, and that they wouldn't interfere with his plans, then there was no reason not to respond to Karrie's unspoken yet clear invitation. At least he hoped the invitation was real, and not something he was conjuring because he wanted her so damn badly.

The problem was, she'd be gone tomorrow. Gone, with no intention of coming back to a city she loathed. It was tonight or never. "Come on," he said. "Let's head back to the car. If you still feel like a drink, there's a bar along the way."

She limped toward him and then reached for his arm. "Do you mind?"

He lifted his elbow, and she slipped her arm in his and the subtle scent of roses reached him. Heat from her body wrapped around him like steam from a sauna. She leaned toward him and her breast brushed his arm.

"You don't have to walk that slowly," she said, her warm breath close to his ear, and he realized that he'd practically stopped.

Few people milled around them. Although the casino was somewhat busy, it was a weeknight and very little activity extended as far as the beach area and the wedding chapel. Even the string of restaurants that led the way had largely emptied out.

He took a deep breath, her scent filling his nostrils, and then he steered them in the direction of the lobby, cursing himself for feeling stiff and awkward.

"Hey." She stopped.

Reluctantly, he turned his head. He guessed her to be about five-eight with the heels, which brought her eye level with his chin. Her gaze lingered on the scar and then she looked up to meet his eyes.

"Is this weird for you?" she asked, her hazel eyes dark with concerned curiosity.

The strand of hair curling against her smooth cheek caught him by surprise. It looked so silky he had to fight the urge to touch it. Press it between his fingertips and feel how soft it was.

"Rob?"

He blinked at her, the sound of his name intimate on her lips.

Her tongue darted out to touch the corner of her mouth and he realized she was nervous. "I won't call you Dr. Philips," she said, obviously reading him correctly. "You aren't my teacher anymore."

"Of course." He wasn't sure where this was going. The male part of him had an obvious preference. Good thing they stood in the middle of the walkway.

As if on cue, a family of four headed toward them and Rob drew Karrie off to the side.

"I know it's a term of respect and recognition, one you've earned, but I think my using it puts us back in our old roles." She paused and audibly cleared her throat. "It creates distance," she added, and then squinted at him, as if he were an errant child refusing to listen. "Am I making myself clear?"

He needed a second to ground himself. He had the feeling that if he answered her this second, his voice would crack like a fourteen-year-old's. At least he hadn't been imagining things. She wanted it. He wanted it. "Perfectly clear," he said, grateful his voice remained steady and cool.

He reached for her, eliciting a startled gasp as she stumbled against him. She flattened her palms on his chest but swayed toward him, lifting her face, inviting his kiss.

Even as he lowered his mouth he knew it was a mistake. There was still unsettled business to work out, relationships to define. Things that mattered were at risk and here he was kissing the woman who could cause him all kinds of problems if this evening of delight turned to one of regret. But the attraction he felt was too potent, as if it had been dormant but simmering for the past six years.

He touched his lips gently to hers, giving her time to back off if this wasn't what she wanted. He needn't have worried. She was more than ready, opening her mouth to him and looping her arms around his neck, pressing her breasts against his chest.

He backed them into the evening shadows and ran his palms down either side of her waist, over her rounded hips. She tasted so damn fine, a mixture of sweetened coffee and mystery, and he forgot they stood in a public place until he heard shrill laughter from a group of passersby.

Raising his head, he saw that no one paid them any attention. A blond woman in her early thirties, obviously a little tipsy and leading her cohorts toward the pool area, was trying to balance a drink on her head.

Karrie glanced over her shoulder and watched the group disappear. She was feeling a little drunk herself even though she'd had only one drink and a glass of wine hours ago. Actually being with Dr. Rob Philips was making her heady. Him. In the flesh. Her perfect Man To Do. Her arms were around his neck. His hands cupped her hips. He'd just kissed her. The whole thing was totally unreal.

Like a dream.

A fantasy come true.

She drew in a deep breath before turning back to him. He slackened his hands as if he was going to release her but she pulled him down for another kiss instead.

His lips were warm and firm and then his tongue touched hers and she forgot where they were or that she was here as a representative for Sanax. Control slipped away and she didn't care. She ran her palms down his chest, longing to reach the hardness that pressed against her belly.

She got to his waist and he broke the kiss. Grabbed

her wrists firmly in his. "I don't live too far from here," he whispered, his lips pressed to her temple.

She slowly exhaled, trying to clear her head. Everything seemed fuzzy. She stepped back. He straightened and let his hands drop to his sides.

"Wow!" she said, her voice shaky.

"Yeah." He pushed a hand through his hair, glanced around. "Look, I—"

She quickly put a silencing finger to his lips. "Don't you dare ruin it."

He stared at her for a moment, and then took her arm and they wordlessly headed toward the lobby. They passed a restaurant and a bar, and then he guided them away from the lobby and around the headless statue of Lenin, a route she recognized as leading toward the garage.

As they passed the Ice bar, she remembered that this was the last place they could stop before entering the elevators that would take them to the car. She slowed and touched his arm.

Before he even looked at her, she changed her mind. She was exhausted, fueled only by adrenaline and tantalizing memories. Oh, yeah, she still wanted him. But the idea of a Man To Do was more provocative than it was her style. Despite her past with Rob, she didn't really know him. She'd been giddy from having him react to her in a way she'd dreamed about when she sat in his class, but was she really prepared to sleep with him on the cusp of this business deal?

It was a crying shame, but she'd better put the brakes

on before things got completely out of hand. It was all too enticing, too easy, and that could only lead to trouble. Damn, but it would have been fine.

She smiled at him, reluctant to break the news. "To be honest, I was going to remind you about that drink I promised. But I think we should wait until tomorrow."

"Sure." He shrugged, trying to look nonchalant but his discomfort was clear. "No problem."

"Yes, there is. You don't understand. I know I'm just one of many students who passed through your classroom. But I had a real thing for you back then." She hesitated when panic flickered in his eyes. Too much information, she decided. "I was young. Basically it was a stupid crush." She sighed, shaking her head as she inched away. "I don't know why I'm telling you all this. Probably because I'm so tired I can't think straight."

"Hey, wait." He touched her arm and then kept abreast of her when she didn't stop. "My fault," he said. "I shouldn't have come on to you."

"You were just reacting to what I put out there, and I'm sorry about that. We have work to get done, and I shouldn't have…"

"No, that's not what—" They got to the elevators along with another couple and Rob stayed quiet as they all got inside a waiting car.

The tense silent ride lasted to the third level where they got out. The other couple got out at the same time and followed close behind, finally stopping at a yellow convertible.

Rob's silver Sequoia was parked only three cars away, and he opened the door for her and waited until she got in. He climbed in behind the wheel and immediately started the engine.

Disappointment gripped her when he backed out of the space without saying a word, and then turned on the radio. The chicken. She thought about resuming their conversation, forcing the issue, but then decided silence wasn't so bad. Maybe they could start fresh tomorrow. Pretend the kiss never happened. Keep their relationship professional. No real damage had been done. Thank goodness.

After they left Mandalay Bay they stayed on the strip, and Rob focused his attention on the considerable amount of traffic for a weeknight. He took Flamingo to Paradise and she could see the Hilton.

It wasn't too late to invite him into the bar. She hated ending the night like this. She'd never get any sleep. At least she could take comfort in knowing the attraction wasn't one-sided. He had responded. In a big way.

Nope. She wasn't going to say another word. She'd said enough. Let him make the next move.

He pulled the SUV up to the curb in front of the Hilton, far enough from the valet sign to indicate they weren't parking.

"Thanks for the ride," she said breezily, and put her hand on the door handle. "I'll be at our branch office and at the county clerk's tomorrow. I expect to have an agreement drawn by the end of the day."

He frowned. "What kind of agreement?"

"Relax. The usual stuff. The property belongs to Sanax, so anything you find does, too."

"Right. Look, Karrie…"

Her door opened, startling them both. A uniformed doorman held his hand out. "Good evening, ma'am. Welcome to the Hilton."

"Uh, hi." She glanced helplessly at Rob and then started to get out. "I'll call you tomorrow."

A moment before the bellman closed her door, Rob leaned across the seat and smiled. "By the way, I had a thing for you, too."

YEAH, AS IF SHE WAS SUPPOSED to be able to sleep now. She pulled on her Donald Duck nightshirt, and then tied her hair back so she could scrub her face and brush her teeth. Taking out some of her frustration on her face wouldn't be a bad thing.

The dry desert air did not treat her aging skin kindly.

She peered more closely at herself in the mirror. Only twenty-six. Looking like sixty, and acting like sixteen. She groaned aloud and then furiously soaped her loofah. How could Madison be out of the country at a time like this. She was going to absolutely die when she found out how close the psychic's predictions had come so far.

Karrie still hadn't gotten over Rob's confession. She would've bet her chance at the apartment on Sixth that he hadn't even noticed her six years ago. Even when she'd forced herself to sit in the first row of his lecture those two times.

Maybe he'd just said that to make her feel better about what she'd admitted? God, she would not do this. Replaying and analyzing conversations always made her crazy.

Too late. Her brain was definitely fried. She kept expecting to find a hidden camera and find out she was the unwitting star of a new reality show. This was all just too bizarre. And she couldn't even call Nancy or Kyra or anyone. Everyone she knew lived on the East Coast and would have been asleep for a couple of hours.

She finished her cleansing ritual by patting extra cream under her eyes and then went to the window and parted the drapes. The strip was visible, bright with hundreds of thousands of lights in every size, shape and color, stretching for over four miles.

What an odd place. All this hustle and bustle in the middle of nowhere. Of course she remembered when the city was a lot more isolated without the sprawl of suburbs so far to the east and west. People asked her all the time if she missed it. She honestly didn't. Not for a second.

She wondered what kept Rob here. Besides his job. He could, after all, teach anywhere. A thought struck her. She didn't even know where he was from. It was funny how much detail she'd made up about him while she used to sit in class fantasizing.

One day she'd convince herself that he was from California, an ex-surfer with his sandy, blond-streaked hair and broad shoulders. On a particularly creative day she'd imagined he was from Australia but had lived in the States long enough to lose his accent.

Chuckling at herself, she grabbed her laptop, sank into a blue upholstered chair and swung her feet up onto the bed. If she couldn't sleep she might as well get some work done.

"Damn."

The gang at Eve's Apple. How could she have forgotten?

She fumbled with her modem cable, got connected and immediately went to e-mail. Heart pounding, she started typing.

To: The gang at Eve's Apple
From: Karrie@EvesApple.com
Subject: Yowzah!
Okay, I know you guys haven't heard from me in a while… I won't make excuses. Last time I wrote I think I told you about seeing a psychic and how she predicted that I'd meet a man from my past. Well, guess what? Stuff is happening just like she said it would. No lie!
The guy is an old professor—he's not really old, only five years older than me—but he was a prof of mine during my junior year. I had the most major crush on him. Really major. But so did all the other girls in the class. He's that much of a hottie.
Anyway, I've just seen him again. Tonight. We had dinner. He remembered me. I'm totally blown away.

Not only that, but he admitted that he had the hots for me, too.

We talked, kissed, he asked me to go to his place. I didn't. Bad timing. But if I have the chance again, I'm going for it.

Did I tell you he has the best smile? Kind of shy and boyish. Very disarming. Because the boy can kiss!! Damn, I'm having trouble typing just remembering. Oh, and great abs! ☺ Don't ask.

I'll write again tomorrow after I see him. Send positive thoughts. I'm a nervous wreck.

Love,

Karrie

She signed off and didn't even consider switching to work as she had planned. The furious and cathartic typing had done its job. All she could think about suddenly was crawling into bed.

Tonight she'd get all the rest she could. Tomorrow was going to be a big day. Tomorrow night even bigger. Because she had no intention of sleeping alone.

4

KARRIE HOPED this was a good idea. If not, it was too late. Rob turned and saw her as she hesitated at the classroom door. He looked awesome in snug worn jeans that molded his thighs, his shirt open at the throat, his sun-streaked hair slightly messy and touching his collar.

He also looked surprised. Definitely not pleased.

Oops.

Only five kids were in the classroom, all sitting in the front row. He said something to them and then slid off the edge of his desk and met her at the door.

He made no secret of not wanting her in the classroom by forcing her to back up into the hall. He closed the door behind him. "What are you doing here?"

"Sorry. I didn't know you were teaching." In fact, she thought the semester was finished. "The department secretary told me where I could find you."

"No problem. It's not really a class." He glanced over his shoulder as if there was anything but the closed door to see, and then stuck his hands in the back pockets of his jeans. "What's up?"

She'd wanted to come and deliver the good news in person. Obviously that was a mistake. "Look, I'll catch you later."

"Wait." He caught her wrist when she turned to go. The sleeves of his white shirt were rolled back exposing tanned muscular forearms. "I just didn't expect you."

"Fine. You're right. I called but got the secretary. I should have asked for you." Feeling awkward because she knew he wasn't happy to see her, she tried to twist out of his hold. Damn, she shouldn't have let the taxi go.

"Come on, Karrie. I'll only be a few minutes. Wait for me."

"Dr. Philips?" A blonde, her perfect little nose wrinkled as she poked her head outside, opened the door wider. "Is anything wrong?"

"I'll be right in, Heather." He motioned her back inside the classroom.

She hesitated, eyed Karrie with excessive interest before directing a proprietary smile at Rob, and then reluctantly closed the door.

"One of your students, I presume." Karrie smiled, already knowing the answer. The year was different, but the female college population hadn't changed.

He sighed with weary exasperation. "Yes."

"Just asking."

"Give me ten minutes. If you want, you can get coffee in my office. It's on the—"

"I remember." She thought about leaving anyway. He could call her at the hotel.

"Don't leave, okay?" He gave her one of those irresistible grins.

"All right."

He winked before slipping back into the classroom. Which would have softened her considerably if he hadn't closed the door again. Hard not to take it personally when it had been partially open earlier. So what the hell was the big secret?

She put down her briefcase and flexed her hand for a second, before retrieving the case and starting down the hall. She didn't want coffee. At three-fifteen it was already too warm. Especially dressed the way she was in a long-sleeved blouse, a gray tropical-weight wool skirt and panty hose. She'd forgotten how casually people dressed in Las Vegas. Even for work.

Still, she was here on business. As easy as that was to forget. Fortunately, she had managed to pretty much wrap up everything. She'd gotten up early and written the press release. As soon as the local office had opened she met with her contact, a nice older woman named Mary, who was so organized, it made Karrie's dealings with the Clark County office a piece of cake.

From all accounts, the land was dead weight. Useless. Not even salable. No surprise. Its only benefit would be the exploitation of the dig. She'd spoken to a reporter at the *Review Journal*, slanting the agreement with UNLV as a benevolent gesture on the part of Sanax.

After she'd familiarized herself with several of the man's recent articles, she'd bought him lunch and flattered him shamelessly until he'd agreed to cover the story, even offering to send a photographer out to the dig. She'd then sent the press release to one of the local news stations and hoped they had a slow enough news day in the next couple of weeks that they might send out a camera crew.

Of course she'd dangled a carrot. As it stood, the dig wasn't particularly newsworthy, and Sanax's involvement less so. So she'd called Mr. Sandhill and convinced him to make a donation toward equipment, and included a vague teaser in the press release about what Dr. Philips hoped to find. Bogus, of course, but that never stopped the media before.

Sandhill was pleased. She'd gotten her kudos. Tonight dreams of promotion and sugarplums would undoubtedly dance in her head. But for now she was a little sorry she'd wrapped things up so quickly. Although if things went well, she'd at least have her Man To Do experience, and given her agenda, a quick getaway was probably for the best.

Sighing, she strolled down the corridor and out to the small grassy area where she used to sit and wait for class, surprised at the swell of nostalgia that stirred inside.

Although she really shouldn't be surprised. This had been home for five years. Closer to Searchlight than she cared for, but it had felt damn good to be away from that place. To her, Las Vegas had been the big city full of promise and opportunity. After she'd outgrown it and moved to New York, Manhattan gave her what she needed, both professionally and socially. Okay, so the dating pool was shallow but there was more to life than great abs, bathroom humor and good sex.

She found an unoccupied bench in the shade and sat down, setting her briefcase beside her. She could count on one hand the number of people roaming around the Humanities Building, so she hiked her skirt up a bit, stretched out her legs and lifted her face toward the sun.

Without the sun's direct hit, the warmth felt good after a dreary winter and reticent spring in New York. She wouldn't stay long enough to pit out. Just long enough to give her ghastly pale complexion a dose of sunshine.

It had nothing to do with the fact that Heather was tanned and disgustingly healthy looking.

The sudden thought annoyed Karrie. What did she care what Rob's students looked like? He'd specifically said he didn't do students. And even if he did, Karrie had designs on him for only one night. Tomorrow morning she'd be on her way back to New York. Let Heather, or anyone else, have him after that.

After another three or four minutes, she realized she'd underestimated the heat. If she didn't want to smell like eau de gross, she was going to have to find some air-conditioning.

She stood, brushed off her skirt and grabbed her briefcase. Laughter and voices from behind her drew her attention. Rob and Heather and two of the others were leaving the building. As soon as he spotted her, his smile faded.

He stopped while the other three kept walking in her direction. Obviously he didn't want her mingling with them.

Perversely, she approached the group. As she expected, he left them quickly.

"I'll talk to you guys tomorrow," he called out and motioned for her to follow him back into the building.

"But, Dr. Philips… We're going to Big Dogs for a beer." Heather stood with her hands on her slim hips, her lips pursed in a pout. Her eyes were incredibly big and blue—the kind Karrie had always wanted. "I thought you were going to join us so we can talk more about Saturday."

"We'll talk tomorrow. You guys don't drink too much." He looked from her to the other two. "I mean it."

Karrie hid a smile, wondering if he knew how paternal he sounded.

"Seth is going to be there," Heather persisted, darting a resentful glance toward Karrie. "He needs to know what we discussed about the dig."

Karrie perked up. Especially when she noticed Rob stiffen.

These were the kids going on the dig? Why the secrecy?

"Then he should have shown up for the meeting," he said, before taking Karrie by the elbow and urging her away.

"He was at work."

"You guys fill him in."

Clearly annoyed, Heather tossed back her long blond hair. "Forget it. I'm hitting the gym," she said, sliding another unpleasant look at Karrie before trotting off toward the parking lot.

"Dr. Philips?"

He stopped, briefly closing his eyes before turning around. "Yes, Jessica," he said, none of his obvious impatience evident in his voice.

"You said we'd be leaving early Saturday morning." She looked young with her brown hair pulled up in a ponytail and wearing no makeup. "How early?"

He hesitated, carefully avoiding eye contact with Karrie. "Seven-thirty."

"Is it okay if—"

"Let's save this for tomorrow."

"Come on, Jess." The third member of the group, a tall lanky boy with hair as long as Jessica's took her hand and the two of them walked across the grass, headed toward Maryland Parkway.

Karrie didn't follow Rob, and when he realized it, he stopped and faced her. "It's a lot cooler in my office," he said.

She snorted. "Confident bastard, aren't you?"

He didn't rebut her remark, or act as if he didn't know what she was talking about, but simply shrugged. "I knew you wouldn't find anything that would prevent the dig."

She wasn't mad. More annoyed with herself. "I guess I proved useful."

"Hold on." He gave a firm shake of his head. "Our history or last night didn't prompt any assumptions on my part. As I said, I knew the land would mean nothing to Sanax and I saw no reason to delay planning." He inclined his head toward the retreating pair. "Todd starts summer classes in a month. Our window of opportunity was very narrow."

She knew he was right. Last night, before he knew who she was, he'd indicated the meeting would be only a formality. But knowing her had made things awfully convenient for him, which bothered her far more than it should.

"I have the agreement," she said, glancing around for someplace to set down her briefcase. "I've signed it. I need your signature and we're done. A reporter from the *RJ* will be contacting you for a quote, and a picture of the group certainly wouldn't hurt. There may even be news—"

"Karrie?"

"What?"

"Can we slow down here?"

"I figured you'd be busy getting ready for Saturday."

"Well, I'm not. If you don't want to go to my office, how about we go have a drink or get something to eat?"

"I have a plane to catch."

His expression fell, pleasing her that he seemed genuinely disappointed. "When?"

She grinned. "Tomorrow morning."

One side of his mouth lifted in a grudging smile.

"That's marginally better than today." He still didn't look too happy, which considerably lifted her mood. "So, what's your plan for tonight?"

She merely smiled.

ROB PULLED UP to the curb just as Karrie walked out of the Hilton. She looked totally amazing in a short green sundress that showed off her long shapely legs. Back in school she'd always worn jeans to class. Damn shame.

A doorman hurried to open the car door for her and she gave him a wide smile that lit up the older man's craggy face. His return smile accompanied a slight nod and an appreciative glance at her legs as she swung them into the car.

He closed the door and she tugged down the hem of her skirt before reaching for the seat belt. "Hope you weren't waiting long."

Rob's gaze was drawn to the soft curve of her breasts as she adjusted the seat belt. "Just got here. Traffic was murder. I was afraid I'd kept you waiting."

"My boss called, which held me up."

"Any problems?"

"No, he just likes to make my life miserable."

Rob noticed a valet parker waving him to move on and he pulled away from the curb and headed for the street. "I thought you liked your job."

"I do. I love it."

"You just don't like your boss."

"No, I do. Really. Poor Herb's been in the business too long. He needs to retire. Which is exactly what he'll be doing next year."

"Does that affect you?"

"I hope. I want his job."

"That's honest."

"No, that's business."

He slid her a curious look. She really had changed. Not that there was anything wrong with ambition. In fact, her confidence and determination were admirable. He was more laid-back. He liked to teach all right, but he liked being in the field more. As long as the powers-that-be and funding allowed him that freedom, he was happy.

"You majored in business, right?"

"Yep. I got my masters here, too."

"Why did you take an archeology class?"

She met his eyes then quickly looked away. "Uh, we won't go there."

He groaned. "Don't tell me the campus rumor mill deemed me an easy grade."

She looked at him again as if she thought he was joking. "No." She laughed softly. "I better warn you that I'll probably get interrupted. One of the Big Cheeses, in fact, the guy who assigned me to this project should be calling on my cell."

He didn't like the sound of that. A call after business hours couldn't be good. "Is it about the dig?"

"Must be. He doesn't normally deal with a peon like

me. But don't worry. Nothing's wrong. He probably just has a question."

He wasn't reassured. "Like what?"

"Like something I snuck into the press release to make the story more tantalizing."

"Such as?"

She lifted her chin defensively. "I merely implied that this might not be a routine dig."

Rob bit back a curse. "Why?"

"Because Sanax could use the good PR."

"You think I'm going to play along with this?"

"Come on, Rob. I could use some cooperation here. You don't have to deny or confirm anything."

He shook his head. "And you had the audacity to act offended because I'd already planned the dig."

She smiled sheepishly. "Okay, we're even." She crossed her legs, momentarily distracting him. Whether intentional or not it didn't matter. His thoughts had already headed in another direction.

"You have any place in mind for dinner?" he asked, his tone gruff. She'd gotten too close to the truth. He did expect to make a find. It didn't mean he wanted the whole city breathing down his neck, waiting.

"Not really. Anywhere would be— Oh, I know. We have to turn around."

Startled, he swerved and narrowly missed a cab's left fender. "Why?"

"I want to go to the Alpine Village. It's on Paradise across from the Hilton."

"Not anymore." He eased into the next lane to make a turn on Tropicana.

"It closed?"

"Quite a while back. It's been seven or eight years. You were probably living here then."

Sighing, she rested her head back and when she angled toward him, the deep V of her dress gaped, exposing part of her breast, and he had to force himself to look away.

If she was trying to torture him, she was doing a damn fine job. Short skirt, low-cut neckline, all that smooth creamy skin. He hoped she was sending a signal because he sure heard one loud and clear. Maybe he should suggest take-out Chinese at his place.

"I had to be about fourteen the last time I ate there," she said and it took him a moment to remember the thread of the conversation. "When we were kids, my brother and I always chose that restaurant for our birthday dinners. They'd give you a bowl of peanuts, and you got to throw the shells on the floor. Of course we thought that was very cool."

"I think I went there once. Mostly German and Swiss food, right?"

"Yep. Rathskeller was the café in the basement. They had the best creamy chicken soup. People used to beg for the recipe, my mom included. But they wouldn't give it up. Said it was a family secret or something like that. Man, I never thought they'd close."

"Speaking of food…"

"Oh, right, um, anywhere. Really."

He looked over at her. She was leaving in the morning. He'd most likely never see her again. So what the hell? Why not go for broke. "How about my place?"

She smiled, the grin at once playful and tinted with sin. "I thought you'd never ask."

5

"WANT TO GIVE ME A HINT where the plates are?" Karrie glanced around the small kitchen, not at all surprised at how organized and tidy it was kept. Of course it was pretty sparse with only a coffeemaker and black toaster sitting on the white-tiled counter. But there were no dirty dishes in the sink and the dish towel was neatly folded over the oven handle.

Most impressive was that the white grout between the counter and floor tiles was spotless. He had to have a cleaning person come in. Or else he was never home.

"The cabinet to the left of the stove. Chopsticks are in the drawer right below." He finished unloading the cartons of Thai takeout and placed them on the dining-room table, before joining her in the kitchen.

"Do you want a fork, too?"

He smiled. "No, thanks."

"Show-off."

"Excuse me." Putting a hand on her hip, he reached around her to get wineglasses out of another cabinet. He lingered, his mouth close to her ear, his hand tightening ever so slightly. "Red wine okay with you?"

She swayed closer. His warm breath fanned her cheek, tickled her ear. "Sure."

He kissed the side of her neck. "You smell good."

Her eyes drifted closed. "You, too."

Chuckling, he drew his hand over her hip, molding his palm to the curve before sliding back up again. He ended up just above her waist, his hand splayed, his fingers brushing the underside of her breast. Her nipples immediately tightened against the silky material.

The dress was new. She'd bought it in the hotel gift shop. She'd worried about the fit, how the bodice gaped slightly. Now as he moved his fingers toward the parted fabric, she saw the flaw as an asset. Screw dinner.

He kissed her again. Briefly. This time at the corner of her mouth, and then retreated. As if nothing had just happened, he crouched to peer into a lower cabinet and brought out a bottle of wine.

"There's bottled water in the fridge," he said. "We may need some for the shrimp."

"I told you I like hot." At her suggestive tone, he slid her a curious look, and she tried unsuccessfully to hide a smile.

"I ordered it extra hot."

"The hotter the better."

He caught her around the waist when she started to move away. "Yeah?"

"Oh, yeah." She laughed, giddy and breathless, and already thinking she should delay her flight tomorrow.

He brought his other arm around her until she was

flush against him and could feel his arousal. "I have a confession."

"You're married."

"God, no."

"What?" She'd been teasing, but she wondered about his abrupt and adamant reaction.

"I can't believe I admitted everything I have to you."

"I spilled quite a bit, too."

"Yeah, that's what probably made me get stupid."

She playfully punched his arm. Solid and hard. "Why was that stupid?"

He shrugged. "Just not my style."

"Then I'm flattered." She tilted her head back, hoping he'd kiss her.

He did. On the tip of her nose.

She was about to protest when he smiled, and then covered her mouth with his. He didn't hurry, but slipped his tongue between her lips and leisurely explored her mouth. Her pulse quickened, and her heart started to pound.

He had amazing timing. The way he went from tasting to plundering made her dizzy. It still didn't seem real. Dr. Philips was now Rob to her, and he was kissing her breathless. Making her knees weak, making her damp between her thighs.

One of his hands slid down her backside and she moved against his hardness, delighting in the low groan that breached his lips and vibrated in her mouth. He let go of her, and she whimpered. A second later he lifted her by the waist onto the counter.

She laughed self-consciously when she ended up with her legs spread, her dress bunched up between her thighs. Rob started at her ankles and then slowly ran his palms up each calf. She sucked in a deep steadying breath, her breasts swelling with the action. His gaze was drawn to her straining nipples, and he bent his head and kissed each one through the fabric.

Her legs automatically tightened around him, and he reached under the hem of her dress, running his hands over the outside of her thighs.

"I had another dream about you last night," he whispered, while trailing kisses down the side of her neck.

"Yes?"

"Uh-huh."

"Tell me," she said.

He laughed at her impatience. "We're acting it out right now."

"Liar." She closed her eyes as his hands slid around to cup her butt.

"I swear."

"Is this all we did? Talk?"

With a deep throaty laugh, he pulled her closer, his fingers tightening over the fleshy part of her bottom, and she held her breath as his head dipped toward her neckline. Using his teeth and chin, he pushed the fabric aside and touched his tongue to the tip of her nipple. She nearly sprang from the counter.

He moved his head back and looked at her with glassy eyes. "So much for our quiet dinner," he said hoarsely.

"I'm not complaining," she managed to say, although she could barely breathe much less talk.

"I've wanted to know what it felt like to kiss you and touch you since the first time I saw you sitting in my classroom."

She swallowed. "Wow. I can hardly believe that. You didn't let on at all. I figured it was all one-sided. My private obsession. Hell, I even remember what you wore. A white shirt buttoned all the way up, neatly pressed khakis and brown loafers. You looked so damn preppy and adorable."

"I looked professional," he corrected, before stealing another sweet kiss. When he pulled back, his eyes had grown darker. "You had on tight faded jeans and a pink T-shirt that ended just at your waist. When you leaned a certain way, I could see a hint of your skin."

"Oh, my."

"Yep."

"I'll have to take your word for it. I can't believe you remember that."

"You always had your hair down. It was a little longer than it is now, and I remember thinking it was a little on the wild side. Wondering if you were, too."

Her mouth opened, but no words came. This was beyond anything she could have imagined. He'd noticed her? Thought about her? Remembered what she'd worn? She felt like a ten-year-old finding out that Timmy Burger had a crush on her.

He touched her hair, letting a curl twirl around his

forefinger. "I liked it. Except it distracted the hell out of me. Sometimes I'd lose my train of thought right in the middle of an important point, which wasn't at all good for my image."

"I never noticed. Of course I barely heard a word you said the entire semester."

One side of his mouth lifted. "I don't want to hear that."

"I studied, though. I even got a B for my final grade. I didn't want you to think I was like the rest of those dopey girls who were only there to ogle you."

Frowning, he lowered his hand. "What do you mean?"

She grinned. "Come on."

"What?"

She tightened her legs around him as a reminder they had better things to do. He immediately responded by kissing her on the mouth. Though too briefly.

He pulled back to look at her. "I had a lot of good students. Both male and female."

"I'm sure you did. But I guarantee you that most of the women in your class weren't there to learn archeology." She instantly regretted the words when she saw how much it bothered him.

"I know a few of the students weren't really serious…." He shrugged. "They have a preconceived and faulty notion about the subject matter. That's going to happen in any class."

"You're right. Hey, it's college. Most kids don't

know what they want until they try it. So there are bound to be hits and misses." She put her hands on his shoulders. "Help me down. Our food's getting cold."

He easily lifted her off the counter. "I think I had a lot of hits."

"Rob, I was only teasing. I'm sorry." She brushed a lock of hair off his forehead, and was pleased that he immediately responded to her touch by kissing her soundly.

He broke the kiss. He knew he was being touchy. His problem. The last thing he wanted to do was ruin their one night together.

He leaned in for another quick kiss, and then reached around her for the stack of napkins on the counter. "Let's eat before I show you my etchings."

She smiled. "I didn't know you etched."

"Oh, yeah."

"Ooh, I can't wait."

Smiling and shaking his head, he carried the napkins and bottle of wine to the table. Why had he thought she was shy? Not that she was overly bold. He liked it that she was playfully brazen. Unlike the new crop of ballsy female students. The way they acted scared the hell out of him at times. The least hint of impropriety with a student would put his reputation and job in jeopardy. He'd always been so careful.

Even now, being with Karrie sometimes threw him off balance. He had to keep reminding himself she was no longer his student. She was an adult, a confident, sophisticated woman who knew what she wanted. That alone turned him on.

She turned him on.

"I think we're going to have to microwave this stuff." She stuck a pair of chopsticks into the noodles and tasted it. "Yep. Where is it?"

"I don't have one."

"I mean the microwave." She frowned when she looked around and realized there was none. Her gaze rested on him in disbelief. "I think you're the last person on earth not to own a microwave."

"I had one but it broke about a year ago."

"You realize that makes you even odder. How could you've not replaced it in two hot seconds?" She carried the cartons into the kitchen, and then stared at the stove. "I'm not even sure how to do this."

"You domestic goddess, you." He got out a couple of pots, dumped the contents inside and then turned the gas on low, while she leaned a hip on the counter and watched. "There. It should take only a few minutes."

"No microwave. Amazing."

"I'd meant to replace it, but then I went to Peru for most of the summer. I got back just in time to get ready for school, and then suddenly it was Christmas break and I was off to Mexico. Spring break I spent in Alaska." He looped an arm around her waist and drew her to him. "It's not as if we have nothing to do while we wait."

God, she smelled good. Her skin, her hair…

She got up on tiptoe and brushed her mouth across his lips. "What were you doing in all those places?"

"Digging."

"Really?"

He snorted. "Really. That's what I do, remember?"

"Don't you ever just take a vacation? Have fun?"

"To me that is a vacation."

She made a face. "Getting hot and dirty. Gee, that's my idea of fun, too."

"If I recall correctly, you volunteered for two digs that semester." He tickled her under her rib cage, making her giggle and squirm.

"And I recall that you excluded me." She tried to get him back but he shackled her wrists and held them to her sides.

"I sure did."

"Why?"

"You were too much of a temptation." He kissed her, lingering, tasting and threading his fingers through her silky hair. He got so hard he had to finally back off.

Her eyes were wide and sparkling, and without missing a beat she said, "Really?"

"Don't look so pleased with yourself." He heard a popping sound and remembered the food on the stove.

"You hid it well. Sometimes I thought you didn't even like me."

He turned off the two burners before he set the place on fire, and then returned his hand to her waist. "I'm

sorry you thought that. I was trying for indifference."
His gaze drew to the tiny dimple at the corner of her
mouth. How many times had he caught himself staring
at that delectable concavity during a lecture he'd been
giving? The breach used to infuriate him. Funny, he'd
been so sure she knew of his fascination. "We'd better
eat."

"Are you sure that's what you want?" A suggestive
smile curved her lips.

"No."

Her throaty laugh kicked his pulse rate up a notch.
She fisted the front of his shirt and pulled him closer
until their lips barely touched, their breaths mingled.

"What do you want?" he whispered.

"You."

He murmured an oath and hauled her against his
chest. Her eager kiss nearly knocked him backward.
Slowly she ran her hand up the front of his shirt, pausing and using her palm to stimulate his nipple. He'd
never been particularly sensitive there but right now
his entire body tingled. If she didn't stop soon…

"Ready?" she whispered, her mouth against his jaw,
moving slowly toward his mouth.

"Yeah." For what, he didn't know. Didn't care. Anything she wanted was just fine….

"Okay, then." Abruptly she leaned back, a teasing
smile tugging at her lips, and then she sidestepped him.
"Let's have dinner."

He narrowed his gaze. "So…that's the way it is, eh?"

"You're the one who wanted to eat." Chuckling, she picked up the pot of noodles, dumped them back into the carton and started toward the table. "This is easier than putting the hot pots on the—hey, what are you doing?" He closed the distance between them, backing her up against the cabinets.

"I thought you liked to play games." He braced his hands on the counter on either side of her, trapping her between his arms.

"I do. But only when I make the rules."

He laughed at the unexpected comeback. "Ah, but you took the lead. Same thing."

She lifted her chin, challenge sparkling in her eyes. "Look out, mister, I have a black belt in intimidation."

"Ah, you're getting me excited."

She rolled her eyes. "You're incorrigible."

"You're right. Allow me to further demonstrate." He leaned in for a kiss but stopped when he heard an odd buzzing sound. Almost like a dryer going off.

"Damn it. That's him. I've got to get that."

He understood when he saw her reach for her purse. "That's the damnedest ring."

"You walk a Manhattan street and you'd better have a distinctive ring." She withdrew the cell and answered, turning her back to him.

He didn't know if it was an unconscious move for quiet and privacy, or if he should take it more personally. At least she didn't wander into the living room but stayed put where he could hear her conversation. He wasn't worried. She didn't seem to think there was a problem, and he did have a signed agreement.

"Sir, I really don't think that's necessary," she was saying, the agitation in her voice sparking Rob's concern.

After a long pause, she added, "But I've covered that with Mary at the office here and—" She stopped again and turned to give him a frustrated look. "Thank you. I appreciate your confidence but really I—"

As she listened she started pacing between the kitchen and the dining room. Rob felt a moment of guilt for enjoying the view while she was obviously distressed. But she had world-class legs. Perfect. Just the right amount of calf muscle tapered to slender ankles. The insides of her thighs were firm yet soft and he started to ache just thinking about them clamped around his waist.

Damn, he wished she weren't leaving tomorrow. Or then again, maybe he was better off. It wasn't as if either of them was looking for a relationship. Even if they were, their lives and careers wouldn't allow it. Better he get her out of his system tonight.

"Yes, Mr. Sandhill, of course I see your point. I think—" She drew in her lower lip, slid Rob a swift glance. "Yes, sir. Of course. I'll call tomorrow with the details."

She disconnected the call and let her hand drop to her side as if in defeat, murmuring a curse.

"Problem?"

Sighing, she twisted her lips in a wry smile. "Guess I'll finally be going on a dig."

6

"YOU WANT MORE of this pad thai?"

"No, go ahead and finish it." Karrie set down her chopsticks. She hadn't tasted half of what she'd eaten so far. Hell, she was so preoccupied with thoughts of the upcoming week that she hardly remembered eating at all. But most of the food on her plate was gone.

Rob scooped up the rest of the noodles but he hadn't been particularly enthusiastic about dinner, either. In silent agreement, they'd reverted to business, discussing the clothes and sundry items she'd need to pick up tomorrow in order to be ready to leave on Saturday morning.

Besides shopping for personal items, she had to rent a four-wheel-drive car so that she'd be able to return to Las Vegas in five days to fly back to New York. And then there was the media angle Sandhill wanted to exploit. Karrie had her work cut out for her there.

"More wine?" Rob held up the half-empty bottle.

"Definitely."

Smiling, he poured some in her glass. "I guess you had plans for the weekend, huh?"

"Not really. Just work. No one's going to do it while I'm gone."

"Well, being out in the fresh air has to beat being cooped up in an office." He gathered the empty cartons, and stacked them and their plates.

She snorted. "Air-conditioning versus hundred-plus degrees. Yeah, right."

With a weak smile he got up and carried everything to the kitchen. "It's still June."

She didn't respond. Hot was hot no matter what time of the year it was, but in a roundabout way, she'd already said too much about his chosen profession. Besides, she was too busy enjoying the view. He could be making jeans' commercials. On the cute-butt scale he was an easy twelve.

"What time are we leaving on Saturday?" Sighing, she picked up the wine and glasses and followed him.

"I'm shooting for seven."

"It's about a two-hour drive, right?"

"Yeah. Then we'll have a couple of hours to set up camp before the sun gets too hot."

She smiled ruefully at the amusement in his tone.

Damn it. The worst part about Sandhill's phone call was that the night had been ruined. They hadn't touched once. Correction. He had accidentally brushed up against her while they were taking the food to the table, and then apologized.

That had pissed her off at the time, but she understood, too. Things had become awkward between them.

In fact, she didn't know if it was her fault or his, but they'd gone from fun and sexy to business and almost formal in three point two seconds. Maybe not completely business, but they weren't ripping off clothes and heading to the bedroom, either.

"I'm still not clear on one thing," he said, frowning.

"What's that?"

"The media thing. Why is Sanax so hot for local TV time? That doesn't make sense."

Karrie hesitated, aware that an hour ago she'd have freely explained about the bad blood between Sanax and Clark County over the government's accusation of excessive water use. Now, everything had changed. And that was the crux of the problem, wasn't it? She had a job to do for her company, and she didn't yet know where Rob and his dig fit in. Until that happened, and she knew they were completely free to explore their personal sides, she had to play things close to the vest. More's the pity. She'd so wanted him to be her uncomplicated Man to Do. One night of bliss and fantasy fulfillment, then a three-thousand mile safety net between them. It would have been so perfect.

Okay, so she was a chicken. Plain and simple. She wasn't prepared to do the deed tonight and then have to face him all week.

They'd have to pretend….

The kids would be there….

It would be horrible and awkward.

She forced her attention back to the conversation,

painfully aware of how the thought of crawling into bed with him blew her concentration. "Frankly, I don't get it, either. I know there's been some friction between the county and Sanax, but basically Sandhill has always been a publicity whore. If he can get the company's name in print or across the screen, he does it."

Rob looked her in the eye. "Bet this ticks you off. Disrupting your schedule and all that."

She thought for a moment, and then keeping her gaze level with his, said, "It does change things."

"Yeah, I guess it does." He passed a hand over his face and then briefly covered his mouth before lowering it. "You'll have a lot to do tomorrow."

"Yeah." She cleared her throat. "If you don't mind, I probably ought to be getting back to the hotel."

"Sure. Leave them," he said when she started to soap the dishes. "I'll take care of it when I get back." His smile was wry. "It's not as if I have anything else to do tonight."

THIS WAS GOING to cost Sandhill. If he said one word about her hefty expense account, Karrie would rip him a new one. Even though she threw a to-die-for long sleek skirt and butter-yellow silk blouse in with her purchases. They were going to look great with the new kidskin black boots she'd gotten on sale at Bloomie's last month. If Sandhill didn't like it, that was tough. She'd packed for a two-day trip to Vegas. Not an entire week.

She shoved the three new pairs of denim shorts into

the duffel bag she'd purchased along with all the other outdoor clothes she'd need for the next five days.

Generally she liked to shop. For silk blouses, soft cashmere blazers, fun weekend tops or snappy capris. Definitely not hiking boots, bulky socks, T-shirts and shorts.

Oh, God, shorts. The thought alone made her want to puke. Her pasty white legs were going to look like hell in them. The alternative, jeans in the middle of the desert in hundred-degree heat, made the choice a no-brainer.

So, her vanity would suffer. She could handle that. What really bothered her was that last night had ended on such an anticlimactic note. On the drive back to the Hilton their conversation had remained neutral. Which wasn't bad in itself except that the tension had been thicker than a two-inch steak.

When they'd stopped, she thought about giving him a brief kiss, but he seemed so anxious to drop her off that she hadn't dared. Her gaze drew to the phone, just as it had several times since she'd returned to her room, as if the message light would miraculously start blinking.

He hadn't called once. She knew he was busy loading equipment for their early start tomorrow, but she'd hoped he might call to meet for dinner.

She glanced at her watch. That was obviously so not going to happen. Resigned, she opened a bag of chips she'd picked up in the gift shop along with a can of cola.

She was in major need of therapy. More than just greasy salty chips. So she opened her laptop and signed on.

She checked e-mail and found that two of the girls from Eve's Apple had responded. The first was a brief note from Susan wishing her luck. The second was from Tori who'd recently married her guy.

Karrie popped a chip into her mouth, set her cola within easy reach and then got comfortable before she opened Tori's e-mail. The latest member to have tied the knot, Tori was still in the Pollyanna phase about the whole marriage thing. Her notes weren't exactly preachy, but she was way too optimistic as far as Karrie was concerned. Of course Tori lived in Houston. Let her try to get a serious date in Manhattan.

Still, Karrie had to admit, the excited tone of Tori's e-mails since she'd married her Man To Do inspired hope, but also made her a little wistful at times. It wasn't as if Karrie thought about marriage and kids all the time. Hardly at all, really. But a girl liked to have options.

She smiled at Tori's screen name, remembering how her online friend had joined Eve's Apple using the alias Angel. She hadn't wanted to be identified. After she'd found Jake, she didn't care if the whole world knew.

Karrie sighed. Would she ever feel like that? She gobbled a few more chips and started reading.

To: Karrie
From: Angel@EvesApple.com
Subject: New adventures and MEN!

Karrie!! Wow!! Amazing about the psychic. Kind of unsettling, isn't it? What else did she say? Any trips down the old aisle in your future? ☺ Just kidding. I don't believe in that stuff. But still… Sheesh!

I read your e-mail kind of late so by now you've had your night. In fact, that earthquake we felt here in Houston…did that have anything to do with you? <G>

Groaning with frustration, Karrie stopped reading for a moment and shoved a few more potato chips in her mouth. It wasn't Tori's fault that last night had gotten screwed up. Her gaze was drawn to the phone again.

She could call him. Nope. She wasn't going to do that. She'd see him tomorrow morning. That was soon enough. After adjusting the pillow behind her back, she resumed reading the e-mail.

Seriously, I hope there were fireworks. That being with him was everything you imagined. What a trip. I started thinking about some of my undergrad profs. Most of them were older and kind of stodgy. But there's one I would've done in a heartbeat. Pre-Jake, of course. Well, as I'm sure the rest of the guys are, I'm looking forward to hearing the details. Come on. We're counting on you. Spare us nothing.

Hugs,

Tori

It could've been worse, Karrie decided as she polished off the rest of the chips. The newly married member could get really annoying when they got into how the group didn't believe love could happen, yada yada.

She used a tissue to wipe the slickness from her hands, as always, mentally kicking herself for putting that greasy crap in her body just because she felt sorry for herself. Although that probably wouldn't stop her from raiding the minibar supply of munchies. But first…

To: The Gang at Eve's Apple
From: Karrie@EvesApple.com
Subject: Man to Do on hold.
Hey, Tori, Susan, et al. Yes, it's true. With deep sadness I regret to report that last night was a complete dud. My idiot boss has extended my trip here. I was supposed to have left this morning after the big night. But now I'll be hanging around for another five days. And no, the postponement isn't about me being a chicken. Not totally, anyway. It's more complicated. I have to get business out of the way first. Really. And then he's all mine.
One bad thing—I have to go camping for five days!!! In the friggin' broiling desert. Don't ask.
Yes, he'll be there, too, but aaargh!!!
I'll write as soon as I get back. Assuming I haven't shriveled up and died of heat stroke.
Love,
Karrie, who's definitely not an outdoor kind of gal, in case you haven't gotten the whole morbid picture.

"WHY IS SHE GOING WITH US?"

"You know why." Jessica had the good manners to speak more quietly, even though Karrie could still hear them.

"I know what Dr. Philips said, but I don't get it. We don't need a sixth person. It ruins everything."

"Shut up, Heather. You're being rude."

Wearing cutoffs so short you could see the swell of her cheeks, the blonde threw a sleeping bag into the back of the green SUV, muttering something Karrie couldn't hear. Frankly, she wasn't interested in what Heather had to say, but she did wonder what Rob had told them about her.

She hadn't seen him yet. She'd pulled her rented car into the university parking lot five minutes ago. The place was nearly deserted so it wasn't hard to spot the trio transferring equipment and bags from their own cars to Rob's Sequoia.

Jessica and Todd had both been cordial, even offering to help load the tent Rob had loaned her. She hadn't met Seth yet. He was late. And of course, Heather had been bitchy from the moment Karrie showed up. No mystery. The girl was interested in Rob, and she viewed Karrie as competition.

Karrie was trying really hard not to be smug. If Heather only knew…

"Morning."

At the sound of Rob's voice, she turned around. "Hey."

His hair was still damp. He hadn't shaved. The light

blue T-shirt fit snugly around his biceps and hung loose over a pair of army-green cargo shorts. She swallowed. Great legs. The kind of muscled calves that always made her look twice. Damn it. This wasn't fair. Did he have any idea how tempting he looked?

She realized she was staring and quickly looked away. Right at Heather, who hadn't missed a thing.

"Did you get the tent and sleeping bag?" he asked, his gaze briefly straying to her breasts.

She hoped the T-shirt wasn't too tight or short. Only a fashionable inch strip of skin showed at her hips. But she probably could've used a size larger across the chest. "Yeah, thanks."

"I hope you've brought more than jeans." He frowned at the designer pair she'd bought and planned to stick on her expense account.

"Yep."

"Good." He purposefully met her eyes, and with the slightest lift of his lips, winked before moving away.

Her skin tingled. The guy was lethal. One look and she was toast. Concerned Heather was still watching, Karrie pressed her lips together to keep from grinning ear to ear like the silly schoolgirl she'd been six years ago.

Unable to resist, she sent a furtive glance Heather's way. The young woman continued to load the car but was clearly keeping an eye on both Karrie and Rob. Karrie was definitely going to have to watch herself. Not that she cared about what Heather thought, but Rob might.

"Who wants to give me a hand with the food?" Rob asked.

"I loaded the two coolers already." Todd took off his baseball cap, pushed the hair off his forehead and set the cap back on his head.

Karrie shook her head, murmuring to herself. A hat. How could she have forgotten something so basic?

"I've got two more boxes of canned goods in my office."

"I'll help," Heather offered quickly.

Ignoring her, Rob frowned at Karrie. "What's wrong?"

"Nothing, really. I just realized I should've picked up a hat."

"I've got a few in my office. They should fit. Come with me to get the boxes."

As they turned toward the building, Heather hurried to catch up with them.

"Thanks, but there are only two boxes," Rob told her. "Why don't you help finish up here so we can leave in ten minutes."

"Seth isn't here yet."

Surprise flickered in Rob's eyes, and he stopped to glance over his shoulder. "You have his cell phone number?"

"No, we aren't exactly friends outside of class."

"A red pickup just pulled into the parking lot," Karrie said.

Rob nodded, watching the truck speed across the blacktop. "That's him."

The bed sagged with the weight of its load, piled high and covered with a tarp. They waited until Seth pulled to a stop next to the silver Sequoia and got out. Tall, with short dark hair, he wore shorts and tennis shoes but no shirt. He had one hell of a body, too.

"I better warn you," Heather said, leaning close to Rob. "He wants to take his own truck."

"Why?"

She rolled her eyes. "He's taking his telescope. It's huge. I'm sure that's it poking up there."

Karrie smiled to herself. For not being friends, Heather sure knew a lot about him.

Rob shrugged. "No problem."

"I'm not riding with him."

"Okay," Rob said slowly as if talking to a child.

"You can ride with me," Karrie said with a straight face. She almost lost it when Heather's jaw dropped, disbelief flashing in her eyes.

Recovering, she lifted her chin. "I'm riding with Dr. Philips."

"Oh, okay." Karrie smiled.

"We'll be right back," Rob said, seemingly oblivious to the undercurrent between the two women. "Tell the others we'll leave in ten."

"But I was going to help carry the boxes."

"We've got them." He turned back toward the building and Karrie followed.

They didn't speak until they got to the stairs and then Rob said, "Too bad you have to drive separately."

"Just as well. I play the radio full blast and sing off-key."

He smiled. "I'd give a lot to hear that. Maybe I should make Heather drive my car while I ride with you."

She chuckled. "You want her to have a coronary?"

He didn't say anything, and Karrie wondered if he knew Heather was hot for him. Of course, he had to.

The office was exactly as she remembered it. Small, cramped with one too many bookcases and a large metal desk, the top having disappeared under stacks of papers and maps. He had a new office chair, though. Sleek, made of top quality black leather. Had to have come out of his own pocket.

She picked up an archeological trade magazine with a desert scene on the cover. It made her sweat just looking at the picture. Yep, this would be her life for the next five days. Damn Sandhill. She set the magazine down. "Jeez, couldn't you talk them out of a bigger office by now?"

"I like this one."

"It's small."

"It's comfortable. Besides, I don't spend much time here."

She didn't get it. Here she'd practically been calling every other day about the apartment on Sixth so she could get out of her shoe box. Not that she spent much time there, either. But that wasn't the point.

"Try this one." He handed her a tan safari-style hat.

It was big and floppy and ugly but it would do the job and she could hardly refuse. She tried it on.

He laughed. "I think we can do better."

She quickly snatched it off her head. "I don't suppose you have a mirror in here."

He reached behind his desk again, to the wooden coatrack and plucked another choice from a limb. "This one should fit."

With a narrower brim, it was what she called a Gilligan hat. Her brother used to drive her crazy watching reruns of the silly old TV series.

Before she could take it, he set the hat on her head. "There. That works."

"Um, great." She held her breath. He stood close. Close enough that if she leaned forward just a few inches…

He exhaled sharply and stepped back. "This isn't going to be easy."

"What?"

"Come on. You, me, the other four…five days at close quarters. You do the math."

"I'm sorry."

"Not your fault." He dug in his bottom drawer and pulled out a denim baseball cap. "Take this, too. It won't cover your ears but it'll help with the glare when you're in the shade."

"I'll stay out of your way as much as possible."

He chuckled, half to himself, and rubbed his eyes.

"As long as your feet are touching the same sand I am you think I won't be aware of you?"

Karrie bit her lip. That had to be the nicest thing anyone had ever said to her. A grin started deep in her belly and filled her with a warmth she'd never felt before. "I—I don't know what to say."

"Then just shut up and kiss me," he said, and hauled her up against him.

7

IT WAS WEIRD GOING HOME AGAIN. Even though the little caravan didn't stop in Searchlight, they had to pass through it. About five miles before they'd reached the small town, Karrie had started to feel the butterflies in her tummy. Her nervousness surprised her.

As a kid she'd hated the place and couldn't wait to break loose. Now it meant nothing to her, good or bad. She had no family left there. Her school friends had all moved away. Even the convenience store where she used to work was gone. That made her a little sad. Made her wonder about the old man who'd owned the place. He'd always been nice to her and her brother.

An hour and a half later her thoughts were still occasionally jumping back to old times, like sitting on the porch of their trailer, waiting for semitrailers to pass and then pumping their arms in the air, trying to get them to blow their horns.

Mrs. Crabtree from next door used to come out in her hair curlers yelling at them to stop. Karrie normally gave in, but her brother would continue to get every trucker's attention until Mom threatened to take a switch to him.

Karrie uncapped the bottle of water she'd brought and took a sip, trying to keep from getting hypnotized by the road. The landscape had been the same for over a hundred miles. Sand, cactus, boulders and the occasional mesa. Even the traffic was sparse this far south. No place to go out here, unless you were a die-hard camper.

Or a Sanax flunky trying to get promoted.

Of course those last few minutes in Rob's office had sweetened the pot. She wasn't dreading the next five days nearly as much as she had yesterday. Just thinking about what he'd said, about the hungry way he'd kissed her got her heated.

When they'd rejoined the group, she almost tossed Heather her car keys and jumped into Rob's car. In fact, she'd even seriously thought about returning the rental car and hitching a ride home with the reporter who'd be coming out on Wednesday. But she'd decided that was more independence than she wanted to give up.

She turned the CD louder, the air conditioner to full blast. Anyway, it was kind of fun to drive again. She never got the chance in Manhattan. If she'd bought a car there she'd have to live in it. Renting a parking spot was way out of her price range.

Rob led the other three cars and everyone slowed down as he turned off the highway. If there was any kind of road, Karrie sure couldn't see it. On Rob's advice she'd rented a four-wheel drive so she managed to stay with the group. It wasn't easy and she already dreaded the trip back by herself.

They bumped and dipped for a couple of miles and then Rob stopped and they all lined up behind him. He got out, shaded his eyes against the blistering sun and looked around.

About a hundred yards south a small mesa sprang from the sand, kind of odd shaped as if someone had taken a chisel to it and carved out a siding board. Other than that there were only cactus, spindly mesquite trees, scraggly sagebrush and little else. After consulting a piece of paper, he motioned them to get out of their cars.

"We'll make camp here," he said when the group had gathered around. "Everyone's in charge of pitching his or her own tent, and then we'll set up a communal campfire site where we'll keep the food and water."

Everyone nodded and got to work unloading the cars. Everyone but Karrie. She had no idea how to pitch a tent. Not a lot of that went on in Manhattan. As a Girl Scout she'd camped a few times and had to help with the tent business, but it wasn't as if she could remember that far back. The back seats of her rental folded down. She'd sooner sleep there than on the ground where crawly things could get at her.

Like snakes. Oh, God, how could she have forgotten?

"Hey, what about snakes?" she called out, and everyone laughed and went on with their business as if she'd made a joke.

Rob immediately headed for the small trailer he'd pulled behind him and unlocked it. He'd been all business once they'd returned to the parking lot, giving instructions and directions and making sure nothing had been forgotten.

It was cool to watch him in action, all serious and focused. His shoulders looked even broader in the snug T-shirt, the muscles in his arms and calves bunching with the strain of unloading the trailer.

God, he was gorgeous.

She could stare at him the rest of the day. But that wouldn't work.

She glanced around to make sure no one saw her ogling him, and then stalked around to the back of the rental car and pulled out her two bags. With the seats down there'd be plenty of room. The windows were tinted and she could put something up for more privacy. Or better yet, she could share Rob's tent.

Yeah, right.

She would do it. In a heartbeat. But he wouldn't go for it. Not with the students here. That didn't mean she couldn't sneak in after everyone had gone to sleep.

"Need some help?"

Startled, she turned to find Heather standing behind her. The younger woman had pulled her hair back into a messy ponytail and stuck on a red baseball cap. She'd taken off the denim shirt she'd worn earlier, which left her in a pink tank top, snug, cropped, no bra. A tiny diamond stud glittered from her navel.

Karrie shrugged, surprised at the offer. "Uh, I don't think so."

"I meant with your tent." She smiled, lots of really

white teeth. "I camp all the time. I'm a pro at it." Without waiting for Karrie's response, she hoisted the bundle of canvas and poles out of the car.

"What about yours?"

She hooked a thumb over her shoulder. "Done."

Karrie's gaze followed in that direction. Sure enough, two tents were already up. Jessica and Todd were working on another one, while Rob and Seth unloaded equipment from the SUV and trailer.

"Thanks, Heather. This is really nice."

"No problem." She hauled her load to a relatively flat area, set it down and then started clearing rocks.

Karrie helped smooth the surface, not just because she had a vested interested in making the ground as comfortable as possible, but because Heather's peace offering pleased her. Who knew what prompted the change in attitude?

Maybe Rob had said something to her, although Karrie really didn't think he'd noticed Heather's behavior. Or maybe the woman realized that they were going to be stuck together for the next five days and she might as well make nice for the short time.

Or maybe she was booby-trapping the tent.

At the sudden thought, Karrie turned a suspicious eye on the blonde. But she seemed to be working in earnest, pounding in the tent stakes, testing them, and apparently dissatisfied, giving one another swing with the small sledge hammer.

Sighing, Karrie chided herself for her paranoia, but

nevertheless, she'd probably still sleep in the car tonight. No offense to Heather.

Continuing to work quietly and efficiently, she finished the job in less than ten minutes, and then stepped back and dusted her hands together. Surprisingly, she hadn't worn gloves. Or maybe not so surprising. Craving the outdoors was as foreign to Karrie as not liking chocolate, but she understood the type.

As a public relations person it was her business to understand all kinds of people. Heather thrived outside, her slim athletic build more a result of honest exercise than membership at a designer fitness center. She was a lot like Rob.

And totally unlike Karrie. Which didn't matter in the least. Although she fully intended to boff Rob until they were both blind, they didn't need to have similar lifestyles. She'd be gone in a week.

ROB WALKED OVER to where Karrie crouched near the front of her tent, trying to pick out small, embedded rocks. "Did you put on sunblock?"

"Yes, why?"

"Your face is getting pink." He stopped himself from touching the tip of her nose. As far as the students knew, he and Karrie had only a business relationship, and that's the way he wanted to keep it.

She gave him a dry look. "That's not from the sun, it's from exertion."

"What have you been doing?"

"Trying to stay cool."

He chuckled. "Give it up."

She started to rise, and he offered her a hand. The touch was brief and innocent, but it still got to him. Whetted his appetite. Reminded him of the feel of her in his arms, the taste of her lips, the ripeness of her nipples…

He had to stop. Get a hold of himself. The next five days were gonna be torture as it was.

"Tell me it cools off at night out here," she said, using the back of her arm to blot her damp forehead.

"You should know. Searchlight isn't that far."

"I've blocked it out."

He smiled. "It gets better as the sun goes down."

She grunted. "I won't ask how much."

"I was glad to see Heather helping you put up your tent."

"Ah, yes."

His curiosity piqued at her cynical tone. "Did she offer, or did you bribe?"

"I didn't have to twist her arm. She's a smart little cookie."

"Huh?"

"I wondered why she suddenly decided to be so nice, and then I figured it out." She gestured with her chin toward the other tents.

He shook his head. "I don't follow."

"See where your tent is?"

His gaze was drawn to the opposite end. "So?"

"Mine is way over here. Any farther away from yours and I'd be in Nebraska."

Rob noted the distance between their tents. In fact, there was a slight gap between Karrie's tent and the rest of the cluster. Had to be a coincidence. "Someone had to have the last tent. Besides, why would she purposely try to separate us?"

Her eyebrows went up. "You're kidding, right?"

"What?"

"You have to know she's hot for you."

"Heather?" He looked over to where she and Jessica were making sandwiches under the white awning Todd had attached to the back of the Sequoia for shade. "No way. She's a serious student."

"So was I."

"But she's majoring in archeology. She starts grad school in September."

Karrie chuckled. "My mistake. I didn't realize that archeology majors weren't interested in sex."

He knew she was only teasing but it still annoyed him, especially since her supposition was wrong. "Look, lots of students like to curry favor with teachers. Sometimes they need letters of recommendation or—what?" Her smug grin was really irritating him now.

"I can't believe you're this naïve."

"Heather likes attention. Not just from me. Watch her with Seth."

"Hey, none of my business. I just think it's funny."

For it not being her business, she sure had her share of opinion. "Glad I could give you a laugh."

"You're not mad, are you?"

"Nope." He was tired, though. He'd spent a good part of last night with Joe Tonopah pumping his fading memory. If the excavation turned up nothing, Rob would have only himself to blame. He should have acted sooner before his friend had gotten so sick. But he'd figured there was enough time and had chosen to explore more exotic places. He was wrong. And now he owed the man.

"Good. I was only teasing. It's not as if I care…." She shrugged, looking defensive all of a sudden.

He was tempted to throw back some teasing, but the others had started to send curious glances and he decided to let the remark slide. "After we have something to eat we're going to start on the grid. Feel free to join us. I'll try not to work you too hard."

"Wait. I have a question. What did you tell the others about me?"

"The truth."

"Then they know I was a former student of yours."

He winced. "Not that much truth. I told them Sanax owns the land, and that they've offered to foot the bill for the dig and that you're the company's representative here to provide slave labor so that Sanax can look philanthropic."

She looked over her sunglasses so that he got the full extent of her glare. Her eyes looked greener than usual. "You're hysterical."

He grinned. "What part do I have wrong?"

She shoved her sunglasses back in place. "What about the news coverage?"

"They think it's cool?"

"I'm starting a journal—did I tell you that already?"

"No."

"Since I couldn't get a reporter here until Tuesday, I had this idea that I'd chronicle everything that happened. If it's a slow enough news week, he might use it."

Sounded harmless enough. "Pretty clever."

"I thought so."

"How many times you think you'll get Sanax's name in there?"

She smiled. "Oh, I don't know. Interested in a small wager?"

"You'd control the outcome. I'd lose."

"Might be worth it," she said, her voice lowering suggestively.

"Yeah?"

"You name it."

He slid a glance toward the others. Everyone seemed occupied. "You enjoy making me crazy?"

"Absolutely."

He hated that he couldn't see her eyes behind the dark glasses. Probably just as well. The way the sun lit up her hair and glistened from her moist lips was enough to get him heated. He knew what a hostage felt like. Exposed. Helpless. Impotent. Hell, it was only the first day and she was getting him all worked up.

He jammed his hands into his pockets. "You do realize you're not going to get away with this."

"What?" she asked, a picture of innocence.

He smiled. "Wait till it's my turn."

She smiled back. "They aren't *my* students."

"Good point. I'll wait until that reporter is here."

Her smile faltered. "You wouldn't do that."

He laughed. Out of the corner of his eye, he noticed Heather and Jessica trying to get their attention. "I'm going to go get a sandwich. Want one?"

"It's too hot to eat."

"There's fruit and yogurt, too."

"I'll come in a minute. One more question before you go." She blew a tendril of hair away from her face. "Why don't you want them to know I was your student?"

He hesitated, not knowing how to explain his position. Not sure he wanted to explain. "I don't know. It just seems simpler if they think we have a business relationship."

"We do."

"You know what I mean."

She studied him, her eyes concealed by those damn sunglasses. "I'm pretty sure I didn't say anything about being your student. I'll try to be careful."

"I appreciate it." There wasn't anything more to say. No way he'd admit that what he had planned had nothing to do with business.

KARRIE WATCHED HIM walk away and head toward the others. She hated feeling like an outcast. A party crasher.

But that's just what she was. No one wanted her here. They tolerated her because this was Sanax land and the company had coughed up some money to underwrite the dig.

In a way, coming up with the journal idea had been a form of self-defense. She needed to feel as if she truly had a purpose here. Besides, if she wanted to use this opportunity to shine, she had to be creative.

From her peripheral vision, she caught movement on the ground near her feet. She looked in time to see a long scaly gray tail disappear under a rock.

She shuddered and moved closer to her tent. As if that would do any good. She was sleeping in the car tonight for sure. Unless Rob had a better suggestion.

8

KARRIE GOT A COLD BOTTLE of water, her notebook and pen and found some shade under the rear door of her SUV. She set out a lawn chair, made herself comfortable and started to describe what was happening.

It was embarrassing how little she remembered of Rob's class. Occasionally a term would pop into her head, but she was going to have to humble herself and ask for his help in editing her journal before she gave it to the reporter. On the other hand, it couldn't be too technical, or they wouldn't run the piece at all.

Using a grid system, Rob had already sketched a map of the area they'd roped off. Considerately, he'd given her a copy. It looked like a checkerboard, made up of quads, each one numbered. She remembered enough to understand the importance of identifying the areas so that when discoveries were made their locations could be recorded.

She watched the students scurrying around. They gathered hammers, rock picks and sieves while managing to listen intently to Rob as he gave them direction. They were all business, yet eager and enthusiastic, and Karrie envied them. It wasn't that she didn't find her job exciting. She did. Most of the time. But this was different.

Finding hidden clues to the past was like unraveling a mystery, like taking a peek into an exotic private world. To begin to understand the lives of people who walked the same earth she did, only thousands of years ago, tugged at her imagination. No wonder the kids were excited. It even gave her goose bumps.

She took a thoughtful sip of water, wondering how much of her own personal musings she should include. Good human interest angle, she decided, and jotted down random thoughts. Even if the reporter wasn't interested, it would be fun to read later. Anyway, she could always edit if she sounded too wussy.

Leaning back, she looked up just in time to see Rob pull off his shirt and grab a shovel. She nearly choked. Seth had his shirt off, too, and arguably had a better body, but Karrie couldn't take her gaze off Rob. A golden god. Perfect. Breathtakingly beautiful. All muscle and sinew, and if there was an ounce of spare flesh, she sure as hell couldn't see it.

Damn, she should have gotten closer. But nooo, she needed shade. What was she thinking?

Both men started to dig a trench while the three other stood to the side, holding smaller shovels and bags, their gazes glued to the newly turned dirt. Heather crouched down and bagged the first sample. Jessica tagged it. Todd craned his neck to look over her shoulder.

Karrie got up, curious enough to take her mind off

Rob's bare chest. At least for the moment. She recalled some of the initial procedures of collecting different samples from the layers of dirt as they dug deeper, but it was entirely possible they could find something on the way down. That was the thing with digs. You never knew. There could be an ancient artifact buried one foot underneath someone's discarded beer bottle. Over time, land shifted, the wind moved with a steady, powerful force. Underneath the ground she so took for granted might be…magic.

She came up behind the other two women and stood quietly. Everyone was so intent on their jobs that they didn't seem to notice her. It gave her the perfect opportunity to watch the muscles ripple down Rob's stomach and across his back as he plunged the shovel into the sand. His tanned skin glistened from a fine sheen of sweat. His shorts rode low on his hips, but no pale skin showed.

Truly a beautiful sight. But even Heather seemed too engrossed in her task of inspecting and bagging the dirt to notice either of the men. Like the others, she obviously took her work seriously, occasionally pausing to take a closer look, and murmuring absently to Jessica.

Todd took the shovel from Rob, who stood back to look at something he'd found. Jessica immediately handed him a small paintbrush and he gently brushed the dirt away. The other two stopped digging to watch as he uncovered something so small Karrie couldn't really see it from where she was.

He pushed his dark glasses back on his head and

peered closely. A wry smile lifted one side of his mouth as he looked at the others. "False alarm," he said, and lowered his sunglasses again.

A chorus of disappointed sighs, and then everyone went back to work.

Again, Karrie felt a stab of envy as she stood apart from the circle. She quickly shoved the feeling aside. They had their job to do, and she had hers.

ROB GAVE HIMSELF first cleanup duty on the rotation. Tomorrow it would be Jessica's turn, and then Todd's and so on. He'd excluded Karrie and no one had said a word about it. Good thing. He wasn't in the best of moods.

Karrie was on his mind, and he couldn't seem to shake her. It wasn't her fault. She'd done nothing wrong. Technically. But why the hell did she have to change from jeans to shorts? It had been bad enough watching her from behind as she bent over the back of her SUV, but now that her legs were bare… Shit. It was a complication he didn't need.

He gathered the tin plates and scraped off any remaining dinner, glad Seth had brought his telescope because it gave the kids something to do in the evenings. But he'd warned them that they all had to be up and alert by dawn. No exceptions. No excuses.

Most of their work would be done before noon when the sun and heat would really intensify. After that, they'd break for a few hours, then resume excavation around three-thirty until sundown.

"Okay, what can I do?"

Rob looked up at Karrie. He thought she'd left with the others to find a spot to set up the telescope. "Nothing. Go play with the others."

"Grouch."

He chuckled. "Ingrate."

"I'm supposed to thank you for giving me a free pass on the cleanup rotation? It's not as if everyone doesn't already think I'm an interloper and a prima donna."

"No one thinks that."

"Please."

"Actually, Seth thinks you're hot. He wanted to know how old I thought you were."

She laughed. "You lie."

"I swear. Hand me those forks, would you?"

She picked up everything that was left on the card table and carried it over to him at the washbasin. "When did he ask you that?"

"Why? You interested?"

"Maybe." A mischievous smile curved her lips. "How old is he?"

"Too young for you."

"Maybe I like them young."

Dangerous for her to be this close. So close he could see gold flecks dancing in her eyes. Awareness in their depths. "Like to train them, do you?"

"There is something to that," she said, pursing her lips thoughtfully. "But I like my men already skilled."

He really wished she wouldn't do that thing with her

mouth. It made it too damn hard to concentrate. Not that washing dishes was that demanding… "At what?"

"If you don't know, ask Seth." She took the clean dishes from him and started to dry them.

"Ouch. Low blow. Where are they, anyway?"

"They're clearing a spot on the other side of his truck. He says he needs a flat level surface in order to set up the tripod."

Rob looked up at the sky. Clear. A half moon and about a million stars. "It's perfect out here for using the telescope. No light pollution."

"It is pretty," she said almost grudgingly. "I'd forgotten how clear a desert sky is. How close the heavens look."

He watched her stare up at the moon, the graceful curve of her neck tempting him to do something stupid. "It's cooled down, too."

She gave him a withering look. "We won't go there."

"Don't you feel better in shorts?"

She stepped back in a self-conscious way that surprised him. "No, I'm not sure it's worth it."

"Worth what?"

"Everyone is so disgustingly tan and healthy looking, and then there's me."

He fought a smile. "Ah, but no one has better legs."

She brought her head around sharply to look at him. "Are you teasing me?"

"Do I look like I'm teasing?"

She switched her attention back to drying the plates and fell into a stony silence.

"Karrie?"

"Forget it." She shrugged. "It's nothing."

"Right."

She sighed. "My father used to tease me about having skinny bird legs. Guess I'm a little touchy."

"Skinny?" The guy was either blind or an ass. "When was that?"

"He left when I was nine."

"That's tough, I know. My parents are divorced, too."

"No, mine didn't divorce. He really just left. Got up one Saturday morning and said he couldn't live in Searchlight and be burdened with a wife and two kids."

Rob didn't say anything, just watched her stack the dried plates and then start on the utensils. She seemed remarkably unfazed. Or maybe she'd learned to put up a good front. It had to have been devastating for a child that age to be abandoned by a parent.

Even though his folks had divorced when he was twelve, they both remained equally involved in his life. During his adolescence, he'd felt they were too involved. Hard taskmasters, both of them. School and studying were all important. No extracurricular activities for him. No Boy Scouts, no summer camp, no school dances. Worst of all was the no sports. At least no organized sports. He'd stolen time and played baseball whenever he'd had the chance, but it wasn't the same as the other kids he'd been in school with. He wasn't the same. But it had all worked out. He'd found his passion. Outdoors, of all things and in the wild he'd so envied as a child.

She looked at him and smiled. "I hope you're not waiting for me to fall apart and tell you what a miserable childhood I had. Ain't gonna happen."

He smiled back. "Not exactly. But you are pretty blasé about something that would have been pretty upsetting to most kids."

"More like philosophical," she said after thinking for a moment. "You're right. As a kid, it was upsetting, particularly since I blamed everyone but my dad. Myself, for the most part. But I also blamed my brother for being a hellion. As I got older I realized that we had nothing to do with it. It was strictly my father's problem. He was one of those guys who couldn't handle responsibility. He shouldn't have gotten married or had children. I wish things had been different but they weren't. I don't dwell on it."

He believed she'd really made peace with the circumstance. Remarkable and admirable. "Do you have contact with him?"

"Occasionally, now that I'm older. And he is, too," she added with a short laugh. "More mellow, feeling a little guilty probably. At first, he used to send a birthday card about every other year, and then he called for my sixteenth birthday and we've kept in touch since then. Only once a year, but at least I know he's okay."

"You're amazing."

"No, I'm not." She laughed self-consciously.

"You are. A lot of people would be totally bitter and unforgiving."

"Yeah, like that would get me far."

"But that you even understand that—God, I want to kiss you right now."

Her gaze flew toward Seth's truck. He knew that although they couldn't see the kids, they were there. And likely to appear at any moment.

She smiled. "But you won't."

"You're right. Not now, anyway."

Her lips parted, as if she was going to say something, and then her tongue slid out to moisten them. She held his gaze long enough for him to need a fly adjustment, and then, as if they'd choreographed the move, they both shifted away from each other.

"This isn't easy," she murmured, pushing a curl away from her cheek.

He watched the stubborn lock of hair spring back and forced himself to keep his hands at his sides. "Tell me about it."

She cleared her throat. "Tell me about your family."

It took him a moment to switch mental gears, but she was right to change the subject. Damn, here it was only their first night. "Like I said, they divorced. I was twelve and my sister was thirteen. They shared joint custody so I saw both of them all the time."

"That was lucky."

"My dad's a lawyer and my mom used to teach so I saw a little more of her."

"Do they live here?"

He shook his head. "I'm from Wisconsin. The whole family still lives in Milwaukee, including my sister and her four kids."

"Whoa."

"Yeah, I know. She didn't waste any time."

"At least it takes the pressure off you."

"Right. Mom's always asking me when I'm going to settle down."

"And?"

"I assure her I'm very settled."

Karrie laughed and hung up the towel to dry. "This didn't take long."

"We try to keep the meals simple. The menu is planned in advance so we can keep the number of pots and pans and water usage to a minimum."

"Wait, don't tell me." She closed her eyes. "I see lots of sandwiches in my future."

He watched the smile twitch at the corners of her mouth. Torture to have her here. Harder to think about her leaving. "You got it. You get to skip the second phase after all the fresh stuff is used up. Canned goods."

"Thank God for small favors."

Rob put all the supplies back under the tarp, pulled out a jug of water for the rest of the night and then made sure the tarp was tied down and secure. "We're done. Want to join the others?"

"The alternative being?"

He grinned. "Sleepy?"

"Gee, I've never looked through a telescope before."

"Come on." Without thinking, he'd almost reached for her hand. Quickly, he shoved his into his pockets as they turned and walked across the sand, shoulders nearly touching.

"Tell me why we don't have a flashlight or lantern," she said, taking small gingerly steps around a cluster of cacti.

He should have brought one. But he'd been too preoccupied with the way the campfire lit golden flames in her hair. "It's not far."

"Ouch."

"You okay?"

"I think a critter ran over my foot."

"And that hurt?"

"No, but it scared the hell out of me."

"So you say, 'Ouch', when you're scared?"

"Sometimes."

"Interesting."

"Which doesn't change the fact that there are critters. Running free. Over my feet."

"Poor baby." He took her hand, squeezed it and then let go. "I'll go back and get a lantern."

"And leave me here? Wrong." She wrapped her arms around herself and gazed up at the sky. "There's enough moonlight. Let's go."

He knew this wasn't her idea of fun and he admired

her for being a good sport. He honestly couldn't say he'd respond as well if the situation were reversed. If he'd suddenly found himself stuck on the crowded Manhattan streets for a week he'd be mighty unhappy.

Heather's laughter carried to them and Karrie asked, "If Seth hadn't brought his telescope, what would everyone have done tonight?"

"Read. Swapped horror stories. Later, after we start making finds, we'll be cataloguing and discussing them."

"I meant to ask you about that." She stopped. "I thought you didn't expect to uncover anything."

"You always find something. Even if it's just bird bones or hopefully pottery shards. That's what this exercise is about."

There was enough moonlight to see the way her eyes widened as she took in the information. Even though it was trivial, she was all ears, interested, attentive. Just as she'd been when she was his student. But she wasn't his student now.

After a quick glance toward the darkness where the kids were, he turned back and did what he'd wanted to do all evening. He lowered his head and brushed his lips across hers.

Her eyes closed, she tilted her head back farther, letting him do all the work. He drew his tongue across the seam of her lips and she eagerly opened to him. He dove in. For just one taste. Just one.

She put her arms around his neck and he slid his palms over her backside to the hem of her shorts, bunching the material so that he could curl his fingers underneath and touch her soft flesh.

Heather's burst of laughter reminded him this was risky business and he reluctantly lowered his hands. It took a moment longer to stop kissing her.

She opened her eyes and sighed. "Tease."

"Well, I did a number on myself, too." He shifted against his tightened fly.

She stepped back and smoothed her hair. "Are we going to have any time by ourselves?"

"Tomorrow."

"What happens tomorrow?"

"We'll go to the river."

"River!" She sputtered in her excitement. "What river?"

"What do you mean what river? You grew up here." They started walking again.

"The Colorado river? It runs near here?"

He laughed. "I see geography wasn't your favorite subject."

"Of course I know the Colorado but…" She shook her head. "I didn't think we were that close…."

"About five miles. Certainly not walking distance in this heat. During our afternoon break we'll take turns driving over there in pairs. I don't like leaving the site unattended."

"Out here? Why?"

He shrugged. "Why take the risk of getting something stolen or vandalized?"

"True. And I must admit, I like the going in pairs part."

"Me, too." He touched her cheek with the back of his hand, amazed at the smooth silkiness even after being outside all day. "We'll have to be sneaky about getting paired up."

"You're the teacher. You call the shots."

"Yeah, right."

She pressed her cheek against his hand. "I can't wait."

"I know." He withdrew, fearing he'd get stupid and kiss her again. "Come on, before they send the dogs after us."

She sighed with exasperation. "Okay. Tomorrow. You and water. Oh my God, I'm all atwitter."

He laughed. "At least I made first billing."

"Oh, yeah. But I dunno, a bath sounds awfully good about now."

"Uh, don't get your hopes up too high. The river can be pretty muddy."

She'd taken only three steps and stopped again. "Seriously?"

"Yep." He pulled her along. "At least you'll still have me."

9

SINCE NO ONE SEEMED to be in a hurry to break, including Rob, Karrie offered to make lunch. She threw together ham-and-cheese sandwiches, set out a bowl of fruit and opened a bag of corn chips, and put everything out on a table under the canopy Todd and Seth had erected.

They'd all eaten a good size breakfast. With the heat so intense, they knew they wouldn't care to eat much in the middle of the day. She called out that lunch was ready, the sun scorching her bare arm as she stepped out of the shade.

Jessica waved that they'd heard her but no one seemed anxious to leave their quads. Karrie poured tins of water and then nibbled on a chip while she watched them slowly gather their tools and tagged bags.

Nothing exciting had been found so far today. At least judging from their subdued moods. That was okay with Karrie. She wanted the dig to be an interesting and informative experience for the kids, but she didn't want them to find anything big like a lost world or sacred burial ground. A find of that magnitude would preclude the land from further development and land her in hot water.

Seth reached her first, grinning, shirtless, sweating. "Great day, isn't it?"

"No, it's hot." She handed him a towel. "You should be wearing a shirt. The sun isn't good for your skin. In fact, it's dangerous." She winced at how motherly she sounded.

"No problem. I'm wearing sunblock."

She got him some water while he wiped off his face and arms. "Find anything?"

"Nah, just some animal bones. Sometimes it takes days before you find anything interesting. You should get out there, too." He grinned and winked. "I bet you'd get hooked."

"I don't think so." She handed him the water.

"Thanks. Hey, tonight I'll show you what I've bagged for the day and explain the process."

"Sure."

"After that, maybe we could look through the telescope since you missed out last night."

"Okay," she said slowly, wondering if Rob hadn't been teasing about Seth's interest in her. She sure didn't want to encourage the guy.

"Conditions out here are awesome. No lights to interfere. Even Laughlin is in the opposite direction of the moon and Venus."

"Oh, God, is he boring you with all that astronomy stuff?" Heather walked up, snatched a towel and scrubbed her face.

Seth darted her a resentful look. "You didn't seem so bored last night."

Heather smiled. "I was being polite."

"Yeah, like you know the meaning of the word." Seth grabbed an apple and headed toward his tent.

Jessica and Todd arrived in time to hear the exchange and Jessica scowled. "Quit being such a bitch to him. He's a nice guy."

"Christ, I was only teasing." Heather pulled the scrunchy from her ponytail and shook out her hair. "Why the hell is everyone so damn touchy?" she muttered and, taking a bottle of water with her, headed for her tent.

Sighing, Jessica slid Karrie a sheepish look. "Sorry."

"Don't be." Karrie smiled and held up water and a towel. "Which one first?"

"Thanks." She accepted the towel and roped it around her neck. "I think the heat's making me snarky."

"She'll get over it," Todd said after guzzling half a bottle of water. "You know Heather. If she's not getting enough attention she starts mouthing off. I gotta go take a leak."

Jessica rolled her eyes as he sauntered off.

Karrie smiled, her gaze straying in search of Rob. He was still out there, crouched in the dirt.

"Dr. Philips is checking out what we've tagged so far," Jessica said. "He said he won't be long."

"Oh, well it's not like lunch is going to get cold. Seth said you guys didn't find anything exciting."

Jessica shook her head. "Not yet. Can I ask you something?"

"Sure."

"Have you known Dr. Philips for very long?"

"Uh, no, not really." As curious as Karrie was to know the reason for the question, she didn't want to ask and start a dialogue. She pulled the plastic wrap off the sandwiches. "I hope some of this gets eaten."

"It will. We just need to cool off for a bit." Jessica sipped some water, a thoughtful frown on her face.

Karrie knew the look. A big fat sign of trouble. More questions were on the way. "I think I've done everything I can here. I have entries to make in my journal."

"If you need help with some of the terminology, I'd be happy to volunteer."

"Thanks. Fortunately, a lot of the stuff's coming back to me."

Jessica's eyebrows arched in surprise and Karrie realized her mistake. "You've taken archeology courses?"

"Only for one semester a long time ago. Oh, here comes Dr. Philips." She hurried back to the cooler, cursing herself for the slip. No big deal in itself except it opened up conversation.

She kept her gaze focused on Rob, still several yards away, which probably did just as much harm considering Jessica already suspected they shared a past.

"Karrie?" Jessica's voice was low, tentative and Karrie braced herself. "When you have some time, I'd really like your advice on something." The younger woman glanced over her shoulder in the direction Todd had disappeared. "It's kind of personal."

"All right. Anytime."

"Just between you and me, huh?"

"Of course," Karrie said just as Rob approached. She offered him a towel and water just as she had the others.

"Thanks." He took a big gulp. "Where is everybody?"

"Potty breaks," Jessica said. "Exactly where I'm headed. Karrie, I'll clean up after everyone eats."

"Good," Rob cut in, speaking to Jessica but deliberately meeting Karrie's eyes. "We're going to the river."

KARRIE HELD THEIR SANDWICHES and fruit on her lap to keep their lunch from getting mangled. Only halfway to the river and her butt and right shoulder hadn't fared nearly as well. The way was paved with rocks, sand and sage, and she felt every rut and bump the SUV encountered.

"Would you slow down?" she asked when Rob accelerated over a particularly large rock and jarred her insides.

"What?— Sorry. I had my mind on something else."

"Ya think?"

At her sarcasm, he slid her a dry look. "It's a four-wheel drive."

"A euphemism for S-M?"

He smiled. "I'm slowing down already."

"Thank you."

He immediately slid back into the silent preoccupation that had descended the moment Jessica had left them. Maybe he was worried that she'd read too much into what he'd said last night. It wasn't as if they could get naked or anything. Plus it was daylight.

She knew people kayaked from Hoover Dam to Willow Beach a lot. The more hardy enthusiasts could make it this far, especially if they camped along the way. More likely, though, one or two of the kids could get antsy for their turn and show up. Of course he couldn't be too concerned, or he would've come with someone else.

Admittedly, she had her reservations, too. She'd lain awake last night analyzing the repercussions of getting physical this early in the trip. Sex could change everything. Would she be able to do her job objectively? Although, except for the meeting with the reporter, the important stuff was done. The publicity angle had nothing to do with Rob.

She slid him a covert look. What would the gang at Eve's Apple say? God, she hated not having access to e-mail.

"Did Heather have a hissy fit when you told her we were going to the river together?" she asked, and then grabbed the armrest when they went over a particularly nasty rock.

"I didn't tell her."

"Just made an executive decision at the last minute?"

"Yep."

"Good job."

He smiled. "Hold on. There's going to be a serious dip in a few seconds."

She braced herself, and waited for the bone jarring to stop. "How do you know this area so well?"

"I had to evaluate it before determining whether we wanted to excavate."

"Why way out here?"

"A friend turned me on to the place."

"Another archeologist?"

"No."

Karrie sighed. Was she going to have to pry everything out of him? If he didn't want to talk, he should've come alone. "Keep it up and I'm gonna think that you're trying to keep something from me."

He clenched his jaw and the pulse on the side of his neck jumped.

"I was kidding." A bad feeling stirred inside. "You aren't, are you?"

He smiled and reached over to squeeze her hand. "If we find anything, you'll be the first to know." He motioned with his chin. "There's the Colorado."

She switched her gaze to the scene before them. About two hundred yards wide, the river gushed south, the slightly greenish-colored water a welcome sight. But no way was it calm enough for swimming.

"Good. It's really flowing down here," Rob said as he parked the SUV several yards from the edge. "Not like around the dam."

"Good? We can't go in there."

"Are you a strong swimmer?"

"No."

They both got out of the car into the furnace of the desert, and he pointed. "Actually, there's a small cove at the bend."

"Are you going in?"

"Sure."

She didn't like it. The part of the river she knew wasn't this rough. "If I have to rescue you, you'll be in deep trouble."

He surprised her by sliding his arms around her and pulling her against him. "You mean you wouldn't save me?"

She plucked off his sunglasses so she could see his eyes.

Any misgivings she had melted away. They were alone. His gaze told her he wasn't going to waste it. "Don't go in," she said, breathless with excitement.

"You're worried about me?" He lowered his mouth and lightly touched her lips. "If we aren't going swimming, what did you have in mind?"

"I don't know. I'd have to think about it."

"Go ahead, I have a few ideas while you're mulling it over." He moved his mouth to her jaw and kissed a path to her ear. "How can you still smell so good?" he murmured against her skin.

She'd cheated. While he'd cleaned up and changed his shirt, she'd sponged down and did some strategic perfume dabbing. But the reminder that they'd been away from civilization for over twenty-four hours motivated her to pull away.

"Come on." She gave him a quick kiss and then took his hand. "Let's go see how cold that water is."

He slipped out of her grasp, startling her until she saw him pull off his shirt. Fortunately he took her hand again before she made a fool of herself and started running her palms over him.

He *was* gorgeous. Not too much hair on his chest. Just enough for her to play with. He had to do some kind of weight lifting to get rounded pecs like that. Such perfection couldn't be achieved by shoveling or random labor.

The ground sloped to the edge of the water, though not as much as she would've liked for privacy. Rob found a small boulder that had been worn down until a relatively smooth plane had formed. But the surface was hot with the broiling sun making a direct hit.

With cupped hands he splashed water on the area, tested it and then laid down his shirt. "You gonna take that off?" he asked, indicating her T-shirt.

She glanced around. "I don't have a swimsuit. I'm only wearing a bra."

"Women wear sport bras in public all the time."

She touched her neckline to see if the strap was showing. "How did you know?"

He grinned. "I'm an expert."

"Silly me." She took another look around and then pulled up the hem of her T-shirt. She got the fabric to her breasts, showed the barest hint of the gray sport bra, and then yanked it back down.

Rob's grin turned to an impatient frown. "There's no one around."

She smiled to herself, and then lifted the shirt again, showing just a little more of the bra. This time she lowered the shirt more slowly and hummed a really bad rendition of a striptease song.

Rob laughed. "So that's how it is." He tried to grab her but she was too fast for him. However, she didn't get far. Before she could put the boulder between them, he lunged and caught her around the waist. "Looks like you need help with that."

Giggling, she twisted and wiggled but couldn't stop him from getting hold of her shirt and pulling it over her head. She stumbled backward and then stood there in her sport bra and shorts.

He wasn't laughing anymore. His hungry gaze roamed her breasts, her bare midriff. By the time his eyes met hers, her nipples had tightened and strained against the stretchy fabric.

"Come here."

Holding his gaze, she took the four required steps.

He put a hand to her belly and it took a second to realize he'd unsnapped her shorts. Then he unzipped them, and she helped push the fabric down until she could step out of them.

She should have felt exposed and vulnerable standing in the middle of nowhere in teeny black bikini panties. Or how the sun beat down on tender skin that was normally protected. But the desire and excitement had been building too long and all she could think about was getting his shorts off, having his skin pressed to hers. The feel of his chest hair rubbing against her breasts.

He reached for her but she shook her head and stepped back. "You," was all she managed to utter, and then she jerked the button at his waistband, freeing it before pulling down the zipper.

He let the shorts fall and then kicked them to the side. He wore navy-blue boxers, the front straining with his arousal.

His tan didn't end, even when she slipped her fingers into the elastic and tugged down the waistband a couple of inches below his navel.

Reflexively he sucked in his already flat belly, and she laughed.

"What?" He nudged her chin up with his warm index finger.

"I'm trying to find where your tan stops."

His lips curved. "Honey, you don't pull a man's shorts down and then laugh."

She laughed again. "I totally understand. My mistake. So…" She drew her finger playfully inside the elastic, exposing another inch of skin. "Where *does* your tan end?"

"You'll have to look lower than that."

Her smile widened. "Come on." She took his hand and led him as close to the water as she dared. The slope afforded them a tad more privacy, plus she desperately wanted to wash up a bit.

"Over here." Rob went first, using jutting rocks for

support to get closer to the water. He held out a hand for her to grab and follow.

"I'm supposed to trust you?" She frowned at the narrow path of opportunity. "You flunked rock climbing." Accepting his help, she gingerly eased closer.

"See if I ever bare my soul to you again."

"Sorry."

The water flowed at a fast clip but she could see where the cove made it possible to splash around a little without getting caught in the current.

He stepped into the water first, keeping hold of her hand. "Be careful. It's slippery right here."

She carefully followed his footsteps. "Do you know how much I'd give to be able to shampoo my hair right now?"

"I think you may reconsider."

"Whoa." She didn't have to ask him what he meant. "I didn't expect it to be this cold."

"Feels good."

It did. In a masochistic sort of way. She kept going until the water got up to her knees.

Facing her, he plunged his fingers through her hair. "You washed it this morning. It smells good."

"Pouring a ration of water over your head isn't the same thing." God, the man understood the art of massage. Even the guy who cut her hair didn't make her scalp feel this good.

She closed her eyes and tilted her head back. Taking

her cue, he kissed the side of her neck, nibbling and tasting until he made his way to her collarbone.

There was something to be said for delayed gratification. She'd been wanting him for days, thinking about his touch, the feel of his skin, imagining the way he'd make love to her, and finally, she hoped, she was going to be very well gratified, indeed.

Privacy was still an issue, but getting less urgent by the second. It was too wonderful to have him so close, all to herself, with no students, no Sanax, nothing between them but a few easily discardable bits of clothing.

He pressed against her, and his hard length made it very clear that he was enjoying the moment as fully as she was. His hands ran down her back, inching slowly over her heated skin, and there was no way she wasn't going to return the favor. Only, she wanted to touch that chest of his.

She didn't move quickly, but still she managed to disrupt his teasing of her neck. Her disappointment was short-lived, however, as he captured her lips with his.

Karrie couldn't tell if the rushing sounds in her ears were from the Colorado River or the blood coursing through her veins, and frankly she didn't care. She parted her lips, inviting him in.

He didn't pick up the pace, which was as maddening as it was erotic. That is, until her palm brushed his right nipple, and then his tongue thrust into her mouth along with his sharp gasp.

Oh, the way his chest curved, the soft flesh covering the hard muscle underneath, the rise and fall, the delicate hair that curled around her fingers. She sighed with the pure pleasure as his kiss deepened. The heat from within her matched the heat from the sun as his body rubbed against hers, and she couldn't stand another minute with her bra on. Her body craved feeling his.

She stepped back, gratified at the shocked pout on his moist lips, and reached for the bottom of the sport bra. Just as she grabbed the material in her trembling fingers, she realized what she was doing. Did she really want to make love to Rob right here? In the open, with the possibility that any of the group could drive up any minute? Or that complete strangers could come paddling down the river and catch them?

"What's wrong?"

The look on Rob's face almost made her laugh, his disappointment was so vivid. But it wasn't funny. Not at all. Because she did want him. Only…

His gaze moved to her fingers, still gripping the bottom of her bra. "Karrie?"

She let go. Stepped back. Just one step, but it was enough to let him know that the moment was over, that she'd gotten carried away. "I'm sorry," she said. "I can't do this. Not here."

He ran a hand over his face. Looked past her to the mesa. "Right. Not here."

"I'm sorry, but anyone could come here. It could be awkward."

"Awkward. Yeah." He smiled, and it was so strained it was almost a grimace. "Would you excuse me?"

She nodded, perplexed.

Rob turned around, walked to the river's edge and kept right on walking. His pace slowed, but he kept on going farther and farther. She figured he'd have to stop when the water came to his shoulders, but nope. As she stared, blinking, he slowly disappeared underneath the rushing water. Completely.

She sighed. Some Eve's Apple gal she was. She'd finally found her Man To Do, and he was drowning himself before her very eyes. Swell.

10

"THE KIDS ARE PRETTY TIRED. I think they'll be turning in early tonight," Rob said, his voice barely above a whisper as he walked past her toward the table.

Karrie hid a smile. "And?"

He looked over his shoulder, one side of his mouth quirking. "I figured I'd do the same."

She threw a wadded-up paper towel at him. About to tell him he'd be sleeping alone, when Seth joined them she kept her mouth shut.

On the way back from the river, they'd made furtive plans to meet after everyone else was asleep. Probably a bad idea. They'd almost been caught once, and in the camp itself, the odds were even greater.

Rob looked exhausted after putting in another three hours in the unforgiving sun. And after returning from the river with Seth, Heather had been in one hell of a bad mood the rest of the afternoon. She'd probably stay up just to catch them in the act.

If Karrie was smart, she'd tell them they'd better cool it for the night. Stay away from each other. Let him get some sleep. But she couldn't help it. Even if they didn't do anything but kiss and cuddle a little, she wanted that. More would be great but she'd settle.

"We're playing charades after dinner," Seth told her. "After that you wanna look through the telescope?"

"Oh, well, I don't know. I—" She forced herself not to look at Rob.

"If you don't want to…" He shrugged. "It's okay."

"It's not that." Karrie didn't want to hurt his feelings. "I can't believe you guys have so much energy. After working all day and swimming and—what?"

A slow grin spread across his face.

She sighed. "Say one word about my age and I will hurt you."

"Heck, you're not much older than me."

"How old are you?"

"Twenty." He picked up an apple and chomped into it.

"Dinner will be ready in five." She spotted a look on Rob's face. He certainly seemed to be enjoying this.

Seth finished chewing. "So, do we have a date?"

She raised her eyebrows. "A date?"

His grin turned sheepish. "Figure of speech."

"Let's see how you feel after charades." She chanced another glance at Rob before setting out a bowl of greens and salad dressing. If nothing else, Seth's apparent interest in her proved the kids weren't on to them yet. Or at least they weren't speculating amongst themselves.

She sort of wished Seth would get a clue. He seemed

like a really nice guy, sincere, well mannered, brought up on a ranch in Montana she'd learned, and she didn't want to lead him on in any way. But there was little she could do besides not encourage him.

Todd and Jessica showed up. No one knew where Heather was and everyone dug into the hot dogs, squashed buns and salad, and then found places to sit around the table in canvas camp chairs. The sun had almost set and the oppressive heat had eased considerably.

Karrie knew better than to hope the weather had changed. By tomorrow it would be as hot as it had been the previous evening. For tonight, they'd enjoy the reprieve. Sharing a sleeping bag would be easier.

No. She wouldn't go there. Not now. First dinner. Already her breathing had quickened and she fumbled with the bottle of salad dressing as she passed it to Jessica. Karrie had again volunteered to handle the meal, such as it was, partly because she felt useless and partly to expedite dinner. Heather had cleanup duty. Karrie would even help her if it would hurry the evening along.

Only two chairs remained, one next to Rob, the other next to Seth. She took the one near Rob and avoided Seth's gaze as she balanced the bowl of salad on her lap. Maybe not a good idea. The chairs were too close together. One more inch and her leg would touch Rob's. No big deal except she wanted even that casual touch so much she couldn't concentrate.

The bad part about this afternoon was the heightened awareness between them since their return. She'd taken offense when he'd headed for the grid as though he couldn't get away fast enough from her. Until she realized she'd done the same thing the minute they'd gotten out of the car. Almost as if she had only to look at him and everyone would know what they'd been doing.

Juvenile, really. But she got why he wanted to keep the others in the dark. The more she thought about it, the more she agreed. So easy to forget she was here in a professional capacity.

After everyone had gotten a head start on their food, Rob asked, "You guys learning anything besides patience?"

Everyone snorted, and Todd said, "Man, this sucks. You dig all day and come up with nothing but animal bones."

"Yep." Rob smiled. "That's the way it goes. But when you finally do find something good, you forget about all those days of coming up empty."

Todd shrugged. "I'm not complaining. I totally get it. Still sucks, though."

"If Heather doesn't show up soon, I'm eating her hot dog," Seth said, and everyone laughed.

"Go ahead and have another. I don't want one," Karrie said, and the intimate way he smiled at her you'd think she'd offered to have his baby. That's it. She was keeping her mouth shut, eyes straight ahead.

"Dr. Philips, I do have a question." Jessica darted a look at Todd. "While we were at the river today, we were wondering why we aren't digging there. Wouldn't it be more likely that the Paiutes stuck closer to the water?"

"They did," Rob said. "For the most part, if they weren't hunting. But that land has already undergone a lot of evaluation, and in areas where it looked promising, some excavation."

"And what?" Todd frowned. "They found nothing?"

"Pottery shards, arrowheads." Rob shook his head. "Nothing of import."

"But that's a friggin' big area."

"A magnetometer team from the University of Texas scanned a good hundred-mile radius going north and south of an area near where you swam and found very little," Rob said. "I've seen the computer printout. The only thing it proved is that the Paiutes used the river. We already knew that."

"Why were the University of Texas people interested in that particular area?" Karrie asked.

Rob took a leisurely drink of water, and Karrie got the distinct impression he was stalling.

"I can guess," Seth said between bites. "The old Paiutes used to talk about a burial ground—"

"Around here?" Todd cut in, clearly excited.

"The speculation was that it lay somewhere between Laughlin and Needles, California, but nothing's been found," Rob said finally. "We don't even know if it's truth or myth. The story's been passed down through so many generations."

"Shit, man," Todd said, and Jessica elbowed him.

"How would you like to make that find? Would that be too cool, or what?"

Karrie stiffened. She turned to Rob who remained impassive. Was that what he was after? "What exactly would a find like that mean?"

Todd snorted. "We'd all get our names in the friggin' university annals and maybe even—"

Rob cut in. "I wouldn't get my hopes up. The area has been pretty well scoured."

"Like you said, it's a big area." Seth put down his hot dog. He had to be excited. Which just made Karrie more nervous. "Look at what happened up north in the Carson Sink area with the Wheelers."

"The who?" Heather walked up and grabbed a hot dog. "What are we talking about?"

Seth gave her a sharp look she didn't notice as she sank into the last chair and crossed her legs. Jessica rolled her eyes.

Ignoring Heather, Todd asked, "You mean the couple who worked for the Nevada State Parks Commission back in the forties?"

"Yeah." Seth looked at Rob. "They wanted to prove that people had lived in the area where Pleistocene Lake Lahontan had receded."

"I remember," Heather said thoughtfully. "They documented over twenty caves and shelters, right?"

"And eventually found a mummy," Todd added.

"Glad someone listened to my lectures," Rob muttered to Karrie.

She heard the satisfaction in his voice, saw the gleam of pride in his eyes.

"Yeah, but my point is, no one thought they'd find anything. Even the cave where they found the mummy had been dismissed earlier. In fact, it was just a cleft in a bluff, running about fifteen feet deep and five feet high. Not much of a living space. But they excavated anyway, and found out it was a burial site."

Karrie listened as the discussion got livelier with everyone chiming in and getting hyped up with hopes of a major find. Their enthusiasm was contagious and she found herself wishing for the unexpected. Nothing too major or she was screwed with Sandhill.

But then again, the land as is was worthless. The publicity generated by a significant find could possibly be the land's only value to Sanax. She started playing with the press release in her head, citing how Sanax's generosity had played a key role in leading to the discovery.

Rob remained surprisingly quiet. She moved her leg until it brushed his. Absently, he glanced at her.

"You must be proud of your cub troop," she whispered.

He smiled, his gaze drifting across the young eager faces deep in discussion. "That's why they're here. They're the best."

"You taught them well."

"I'm not their only prof."

"But they like and respect you. I can tell. They learn more from someone like you."

His lips curved in a patronizing smile.

She didn't care. That wasn't her bias speaking. It was the truth. She could see how much the students admired and respected him. And he'd earned every bit of both. He treated them like equals, not like some of the profs she'd had who assumed every student was an idiot.

"What do you think, Dr. Philips?"

He blinked at Todd. "What's that?"

"Do you think it's worth considering moving the site closer to the river?"

Rob stiffened. "No."

His abrupt answer surprised everyone judging by the startled looks on their faces.

"We've done some good work here already. It's only been two days. You have to be patient." After a brief silence, he added, "If it looks as if we're going nowhere at the end of two weeks, we'll discuss moving closer to the river."

Seth shrugged. "Sounds good."

"Sure." Jessica smiled.

Heather sighed.

Todd let his head fall back and stared up at the sky in silence.

If Karrie had had to guess which one would be disgruntled she'd have pegged Todd. They were all so different. As good-natured and laid-back as Seth was, Todd was moody, sometimes sullen. Not a good match for Jessica, who was a little shy but always smiling and optimistic, definitely a nurturer. And Heather…she was just Heather, self-absorbed and used to attention. Definitely had to have been a high school cheerleader. Of course so was Karrie….

She snapped out of her preoccupation as the kids started to get up and dispose of their leftovers. Seth asked who was going to play charades but Todd ignored him and headed toward the tents. Jessica gave Seth an apologetic smile and then followed Todd.

Heather cocked her head to the side and gave Seth a saucy smile. "Help me clean up and I'll play."

"Right."

"I'll help you when it's your turn."

"Right."

"Can you answer in anything but a single syllable?"

"No."

Heather let out a frustrated growl, snatched the bowl of leftover greens from the table and marched off toward the supply tent.

Seth grinned and gathered the utensils and extra napkins. He started to follow her but then stopped. "Karrie, it's too light yet to use the telescope. Maybe in another hour…"

She waved him off. "We'll talk then."

As soon as they were alone, she turned to Rob. He had the oddest expression on his face.

"What's wrong?"

He shook his head, rubbed his eyes and then stared at her with a wariness she found unnerving. "I have a question for you."

"Yeah…"

"If we were to find something—hypothetically, of course, because I don't think we will—how would that affect you as far as your position with Sanax?"

"Depends what you found, I guess."

"Say we did find evidence of a Paiute burial ground." His gaze fastened on hers. "And the State wanted us to excavate further."

"Sanax would have to abide by an agreement the former owner made with the government at the time of purchase. The land becomes frozen. No development or mining or anything else until the status has been determined."

"I know. I'm talking about you. How would something like that affect your career?"

Disappointment sliced through her. "A little late to worry about me, isn't it?"

"Look, I'm not saying we'll find anything. But there are certain myths we can't discount…." He looked past her. Heather and Seth were headed back toward them. He lowered his voice. "I never intended to compromise you. I *won't* compromise you, okay?"

She folded her arms across her chest. So what if the kids were coming? If he didn't want to speak in front of them he should have laid this all out earlier. The first night they met for dinner. "What do you know?"

"Nothing concrete. I swear."

"You're not answering my question."

Heather darted them a curious look but stayed unusually quiet as she finished clearing the table.

"Come on, let's go for a walk." Rob took Karrie by the elbow.

"You guys coming back for charades?" Heather called as he steered Karrie away from the camp.

"No," Rob yelled back.

It wasn't dark yet, but close, and he grabbed a flashlight from the back of his SUV.

"I don't like this." Karrie shook out of his grasp.

"What?"

"Why do we have to come out here? So you can finish me off?"

He sighed with weary exasperation. "I want to explain something to you."

"I don't want to go too far and have to walk back in the dark."

He pointed to a small mesa she'd already investigated this morning, looking for shade and quiet while the others worked. "That's as far as we'll go," he said. "If you want, we'll go back to camp before it gets dark."

It wasn't all that close and there wasn't much light already. "Don't snakes come out after sunset?"

"Only sidewinders."

"Funny."

"I've got the flashlight and we'll stay in the open where they can't ambush us."

"That's supposed to make me feel better?" Her gaze stayed glued to the ground as they walked silently toward the mesa.

Earlier she would have been thrilled with the opportunity to be alone with him. But that was before he'd ticked her off. The bastard knew something he hadn't shared with her. That hurt. Made her mad.

All that crap about how he'd noticed her in his classroom but hadn't acted on the attraction because she was a student was awfully damn convenient. Especially after, like a moron, she'd confessed having a thing for him. Made her wonder how much he'd led her on in order to distract her and gain her support.

"You're quiet," he said after they got there.

"I'm pissed."

"Hear me out before you jump to conclusions."

"Talk."

He sighed. "Let's sit." He brushed off the flat top of a jutting rock and gestured.

She scanned the ground for any lurking critters and then perched on the rock. She hadn't expected him to sit beside her and almost made him get up when he settled next to her, his legs and shoulder rubbing hers. But there really wasn't anyplace else to sit and she didn't want to come off as childish.

"I'm going to tell you everything I know—why I wanted to dig here specifically, what I've learned about the area that's piqued my interest. Everything. Okay?"

She remained stubbornly silent. Better that then blasting him with sarcasm about how this honesty was a little late in coming.

"I have a friend, a Paiute Indian from a reservation north of here. Joe's eighty-eight, in bad health, and it doesn't look as if he's going to be around much longer." He paused and looked at her. "I'm not telling you that for sympathy. I just want you to understand where I'm coming from."

His nearness and his warm breath fanning her cheek elicited an instant reaction. Damn him. How could she still feel even a trace of attraction? How could her pulse quicken, her heart turn over in her chest?

Disgusted with herself as much as with him, she shifted away, turning her knees toward camp. Two of the tents were lighted, but from this distance she couldn't actually see anyone.

"Karrie?"

"I'm listening."

He sighed. "Joe's grandfather used to tell a story about their ancestors' journey along the river, headed toward what we now know as California. They'd almost reached their destination when they were attacked by a rebel band of cavalry soldiers. According to legend, half the tribe was massacred before help arrived. The survivors stayed to bury their dead before continuing on."

"So why aren't you looking closer to the river?"

"Joe's grandfather believed that they'd chosen a place away from the river so that their dead wouldn't be disturbed. He mentioned this mesa as a landmark."

Karrie stiffened. "This mesa? As in where we're sitting right now?"

He nodded, and she shuddered.

He touched her arm. "This isn't where the burial ground is. If my calculations are correct, it should be in the area where we're digging."

"But why hasn't a museum or the University or someone already excavated and found it by now? The attack would have been documented and so would the Paiute's trail."

"The government was embarrassed by the attack. There is no documentation. Only Indian folklore."

"So this could be a wild-goose chase."

"Yep."

She turned to study him in the waning light. "But you don't think so."

"I honestly have no idea. But I made a promise to Joe that I'd search and the experience is good for the students." He shrugged. "I hope we do find something. I—" He broke off, and stared away toward a stream of fading pinkish-orange clouds on the horizon.

"Now is not the time to hold back," she warned.

"I understand." He absently shook his head. "This thing with Joe Tonopah is personal. He'd asked me five years ago to find his ancestors' burial ground. I agreed but then got caught up in furthering my career. I needed to publish in order to get tenured and then I was offered a chance to join a team searching for the Anasazi ruins in New Mexico. I screwed up. I failed him. And now he's dying."

Karrie inhaled deeply. She understood the sacrifices the pursuit of a career required. Too well. It had been over three years since she'd made time to see her mother or her brother. How would she feel if, God forbid, one of them suddenly got really sick?

She sighed. "You still should've explained this all to me before now. I think I deserve some trust."

His wry smile implied he disagreed. "Think about it. How well did I know you until four days ago? You'd been my student six years ago and suddenly you show up as Sanax's rep."

She stared, amazed that it had only been four days since she'd arrived from New York and sat across the table from him at Joe's Crab Shack.

"Yes, ethically I should have told you," he continued. "I know that. But my lapse wasn't personal. If it weren't you sitting here, do you think I'd be making an ass out of myself and admitting what a shit I've been? I'd have continued to play dumb. Let Sanax think I expected to find nothing, and then just wait and see."

She didn't say anything for a moment, and then muttered, "You are an ass."

Her tone obviously told him she'd softened because he smiled, picked up her hand and brought it to his lips. "Forgive me."

Damn him.

She grabbed a fistful of his shirt, pulled him close and kissed him.

11

Karrie didn't know if she believed him or just wanted to believe him. What he said was logical. He didn't know her well, and he could have kept quiet. She hoped her judgment wasn't being influenced by the solid feel of him beneath her palms or the musky scent of his skin.

Or the way his lips slanted over hers, demanding, taking possession. She opened her mouth to him and his tongue delved inside to mate with hers. He swept the soft fleshy part of her inner cheek and then ran his tongue over her teeth as if not wanting to miss a speck of her.

She automatically leaned back with his weight pressing her and he brought his arms up to cradle her to his chest. His heart thundered against her breasts. Her heart answered the call. With a shudder, she worked her hands to the hem of his T-shirt and then slid them beneath, running her palms over his flat belly, lightly tracing the scar with her fingertips and then pressing up to his chest.

He smiled against her mouth and then mimicked her actions, quickly finding and cupping her breasts through her bra. She arched her back, pushing harder against his palms, her nipples aching for his touch.

"Let's take this off," he whispered, sliding his hands out and tugging at the hem of her T-shirt.

She glanced toward camp. No one in sight. "It's not dark enough yet."

He blinked, surprise flickering in his face, as if he'd forgotten where they were. "Come here."

As soon as he took her hand, she knew where he was leading her. She'd seen the other side of the mesa earlier today. Far from ideal, but the shallow cleft did provide some privacy and a decent place to sit.

"Ten more minutes and it'll be dark," he said backing her up against the rock wall and kissing the side of her neck, tugging at her hem.

"Someone might come looking for us."

"Doubt it."

"Anyway, we'd hear them. Right?"

"Uh-huh."

She didn't know if she even believed that herself but she raised her arms and he pulled off her shirt, and then quickly got rid of his. He didn't hesitate to push up her sport bra and expose both breasts.

He stared appreciatively for a moment, nostrils flaring slightly before taking a nipple into his mouth. She closed her eyes and ignored the rock wall against her back. She could barely think of anything except the greedy way he suckled her, easing off at just the right instant, and then increasing the pressure for another round until he'd rendered her breathless and aching.

Finally, he eased back, his gaze going to her ripe wet nipples. "I wanna get naked," he murmured and briefly touched his tongue to the tip of one as if he couldn't help himself. Just had to taste her one more time.

She smiled, feeling a little dizzy at the thought. "How safe do you think it would be in one of our tents after everyone goes to sleep?"

"I dunno." One side of his mouth went up and he slid a finger under the waistband of her shorts, casually rubbing back and forth. "I was hoping to make you scream."

She shivered. At this point, that wouldn't take much. Being hot and bothered for four days was some foreplay. Getting up on tiptoe, she nipped the end of his stubbled chin. "I figure you'll do some screaming yourself."

"Baby, I wanna scream now." He cupped her backside and moved his hips against her, his arousal hard and tempting.

"This is going to be awkward," he murmured.

"I don't care." She didn't care about a lot of things. The way he made her quiver, the entire group of students could have climbed up on the mesa with binoculars, and she wouldn't have missed a beat. To show him, she ran her hand down the front of his shorts.

Her reward was his hard length, aching so pressingly for her, for this.

He moaned, then buried his mouth against her neck. He kissed her there while he pressed against her hand.

His hands, meanwhile, went to her breasts, teasing her nipples with the tips of his fingers.

Her eyes rolled back as she leaned against the warm rock behind her. It was hard to tell who was panting harder. His hot breath against her neck was different from the air. Moist, intimate.

God, she was leaning against a rock with Rob Philips. How many nights had this been her dream? Well, maybe not the rock, and definitely not the desert and there'd always been champagne, but other than that, it was just as she'd always imagined it. Okay, maybe her imagination hadn't been quite generous enough when it came to his assets, but that could be forgiven. His lips, though. They'd been this perfect, this tender and hot, all at the same time. His hands, so rough from his work, were just calloused enough to rub her to madness, and that was something totally unexpected.

His right hand dipped, leaving her nipple to make its own friction by rubbing his chest, but making up for it by slinking beneath her shorts.

He pushed them down, never ceasing the action with his left hand, until he'd bared her almost to the top of her soft curls.

"Karrie," he whispered, moving his lips across her chin, kissing her softly, tenderly. But when he reached her mouth, the tenderness turned to fire, burning her hotter than any flame.

Somehow, she found the button at the top of his shorts, and while her hand was a trembling mess, she got it undone. The zipper was trickier, but she was determined. Especially when she felt her own shorts slip down her legs to puddle on her sandals.

"Oh, God," he whispered. "I can't believe this is really happening."

"I know."

"I thought about this. About you."

"You did?"

He nodded, nipping her lower lip. "You made me crazy back then. But it was nothing like this."

"I made you crazy?"

He chuckled, a deep, sexy sound that made his chest vibrate wonderfully. "God, yes. But I couldn't, didn't dare."

"No, of course not. You were so…"

"Yeah. So…"

"But now."

"Now," he said, his lips teasing the lobe of her ear, giving her the shivers. "Now, I've got you."

She moved her hands to his ass, and that's when his shorts fell away. Leaving him as naked as she was.

The sky had turned a brilliant red as the sun dipped beneath the horizon. His hands ran over her body, touching her everywhere except the one place that needed him the most.

Brazenly, she spread her legs as she wrapped her fingers around his length.

He cursed with her touch, as she found his moisture and rubbed it all the way up to the base.

"You don't like that?"

Through gritted teeth, he said, "I love that. Only, my pants are way down there."

"Your pants?"

He nodded. "The pocket."

She didn't understand for a second, and then she did. The pocket. She let go.

Rob gasped, held very still for one long second, then bent to get the silver packet hidden in his wallet. Being the terribly creative man he was, he didn't waste the position. She felt hands brace her hips. It was a good thing she was leaning against the rock, because she would have fallen at his next move.

He moved very, very close. So close, he touched her lower lips with the tip of his tongue. Then it wasn't her lips, but the swollen bud, and she had to bite her own lip to stop from screaming.

Her hands went to his hair, gripping him tightly, as he circled and circled, until she thought she would go insane. Her body started tensing, that familiar yet illusive pressure built from the toes up her toes, to her thighs. Then spread to her chest, her breasts, zeroing in on her nipples, making her forget how to breathe, how to see.

He stopped circling. Instead, he hardened his tongue and touched her just there, the exact spot, the bull's-eye, the magic button, and in two hot seconds, she was a goner.

She couldn't hold back the sounds, although she tried, but it was out of her control. She came. Came so hard, she practically ripped his hair out of his head.

She was still vibrating when he stood, and out of the corner of one slightly blurred eye, she saw him rip open the condom. Her eyes closed again, and she sank back farther on the rock, not caring in the least that it was sharp and hot.

His hands came back to her hips, and one of his feet moved her leg to the right. Then, when she was still trembling like a leaf, he entered her.

The only thing that stopped this scream was his mouth on hers. Kissing. Hard. Thrusting above and below. Taking her, marking her, making her moan to her toenails.

He filled her completely, and the way he was positioned, the way he rubbed her, was amazing. Because as he pushed in and out, the pressure began all over again. She was heading for another climax when she'd barely finished the first.

Kissing him wasn't enough, but it was all she could do. She felt helpless, like jelly in his arms. Pinioned against the rock in the middle of the desert, she was consumed by the bliss of her body while her mind was blown by the dream come true.

He pulled back, his rhythm quickening, and she knew he wouldn't last much longer. She wanted him to explode, to feel what she felt. She thrust back at him, and that was it.

His head reared back revealing the tendons in his neck, the pulse at his temple, and his mouth opened in a silent roar. So powerful was his release that he actually lifted her for a moment. And then he breathed again, falling against her, panting and gasping.

She couldn't speak. But then, neither could he. They didn't need to.

It might have been awkward, outside, and there had been no champagne. But hot damn, he wasn't just a Man To Do. He was the Man Who Made Her Dreams Come True. But good.

"HAVE YOU GOT A MINUTE, Dr. Philips?" Heather had barely waited for him to take the last bite of his sandwich. "I need help with something."

"Sure." He drank the rest of his water and got up, sliding Karrie a brief glance she couldn't interpret.

Were they going to the river today? Or was he going to spend the afternoon studying samples instead? Hard to tell. He hadn't uttered more than "good morning" and "thanks for making lunch" today. Mostly because Heather hadn't given him enough time.

She'd monopolized him from the moment she stepped out of her tent this morning. Always needing to discuss something dig related, however small and insignificant, she managed to capture his attention.

"I found something this morning I'm having trouble identifying," Heather said with a pathetically transparent smile as she led him toward the open tent where they stored and cataloged their finds.

Rob didn't seem disturbed or even cognizant of Heather's sudden attention-demanding tactics ever since last night, after he and Karrie had returned to the camp and joined the others. He merely followed Heather, grabbing another bottle of water on the way.

Hard to believe he could be that naive, or maybe he'd decided if he stayed cool and professional, Heather would finally get a clue. He hadn't encouraged her. Of course he hadn't discouraged her, either.

With mixed feelings, Karrie watched them disappear. To some degree she was glad for the space. Time to think about what happened between them last night. As if she hadn't spent half the night, tossing and turning, incredulous that she could feel so many conflicting emotions at once.

Damn, she wasn't supposed to care this much about him. It had only been sex, right? A fantasy come true. That's all. Simple. Really.

So why did she want to rip Heather's heart out for soaking up his time like a damn sponge? Of course that was an unreasonable desire that had nothing to do with possessiveness or jealousy, or anything other than the fact that Karrie had a limited amount of time left with Rob. And the sex had been great. Fantastic.

Amazing how he seemed to know exactly how she liked to be touched as if they'd been a couple for years. Everything he'd done and made her feel was perfect. So of course she had every right to resent Heather's interference without overanalyzing the reason. It was all about great sex. Period.

"Karrie?" Jessica brought out a trash bag and started

clearing the lunch remnants. "Todd's gone to our tent to take a quick nap. I was wondering if you had time to—remember I'd asked you if we could talk sometime?"

"Come on. Let's go find some shade away from here. In fact, let's treat ourselves and go sit in my car with the air conditioner going full blast."

Jessica darted a look toward her tent. "I didn't want anyone to see us talking. I mean, I don't want it to look like it's anything but a casual conversation."

Karrie picked up the notebook she carried with her most of the time and winked. "Don't forget you promised me that interview. Please, step into my office." She gestured toward her rental.

It sounded like a good idea. In reality, the inside of the car was too damn hot to cool down quickly enough. Today was easily the hottest day yet. Just being out in the blistering sun for the minute it took to get to the car, Karrie felt her skin prickle with the heat.

She left the ignition turned on and the air going on high, hoping it would eventually cool down enough for them to crawl in and get some relief.

"How do you guys stand this?" she asked Jessica who waited patiently near the driver's door.

Her dark eyebrows drew together under her floppy safari hat. "What?"

"Being out in this heat. Standing under the hot sun most of the day."

Her eyes lit up. "It's totally worth it. To find that one

tiny link to history is so awesome, it's like…" She spread her hands. "I can't even describe the feeling. It's the best high."

Karrie smiled at the other woman's animation. "I think I might be beginning to understand. Heck, even I get excited when you guys are out there and I see one of your heads come up quickly."

Jessica giggled. "Yeah, it could be the dusty top of a pop can and we all go running to see."

They'd had a couple of false alarms. Excitement had turned to disappointment and then everyone had returned to work. No one seemed to get discouraged, though. The whole cycle was pretty interesting. Certainly not another day at the office.

"So, kiddo, what did you want to talk about?"

Jessica stared down at her worn tennis shoes, and then slanted a look toward the open canopy where everyone normally congregated. "It seems kind of silly now that we're standing out here."

"Come on."

Jessica sighed, hesitated another moment. "It's about Todd and me. I don't think he's as serious about our relationship as I am."

Karrie wasn't sure how to respond to that, but Jessica paused. "How long have you been going out?"

"Eight months." She shrugged. "I know that's not long, but— Oh, God, this is so embarrassing." She paused, and then in a rush said, "I think he's just in it for the sex."

"Ah." Karrie's brilliance stopped there. She was so not the right person to be asking advice about this. That's all she wanted from Rob. Of course that's all it could be for them. They were headed down different paths. He had ties to UNLV, and she was going places with Sanax.

After a brief silence, Jessica said, "You're probably going to tell me to dump him. He's not the most congenial person on earth. My parents can't stand him. And they haven't even met him in person yet. They've just talked to him on the phone."

Karrie smiled. "I'm not going to tell you to dump him. No one can tell you that. You have to decide for yourself."

"But I don't want us to keep going this way, either. Half the time we don't even look like we're a couple. He rarely holds my hand or acts like he cares. He never asks about how my day was, or if I'd like to go out. We're either at home, at school or Big Dogs. I hate it."

"Have you talked to him?"

Jessica snorted. "You mean, asked him if all he wants is sex?"

"Yeah." Karrie smiled at Jessica's look of horror. "Not that blatantly, of course. But sit him down and ask him what he wants. Where he sees himself in the next five years. Where he sees the two of you. More important, make it clear to him what *you* want."

Jessica slowly shook her head. "He won't want to talk. He'll cut me off after the first sentence."

"Then you make sure the first thing you say is that avoiding the conversation is a deal breaker for the relationship."

Jessica flinched.

"I know. Easy for me to say. But you asked."

"You're right." The younger woman took a deep breath. "I'm such a wimp."

Karrie laughed softly. "We all are when it comes to this kind of stuff. Easier for me to be standing on this side of the fence giving advice. But it all comes down to what will make you happier. Will it be staying with him under these conditions, or taking the risk and being prepared to walk away if things don't improve?"

Jessica's heartfelt sigh was followed by a groan. "Oh, God, this sucks."

"Amen."

"I'll talk to him." Her mouth lifted in a wry smile. "Can I share your tent if he kicks me out?"

"He might surprise you."

"Maybe." She drew her palms down her baggy cargo shorts, then took off her sunglasses and rubbed her eyes before replacing the glasses. "Guys can be so clueless."

So were a lot of women, but Karrie wasn't going there. "The car's cool enough now."

"I'd better get back."

"If anyone asks I was doing the interview thing."

"Thanks." Jessica smiled. "Tonight. I'm doing it. For sure."

That was gutsy. Karrie probably would've waited

until the last day. But she was keeping her mouth shut. She'd given more than her two cents already.

Jessica rolled her shoulders and then straightened, as if preparing for battle. "Wish me luck."

"Luck."

"Coming or staying?"

"The car's finally cool. I'm not wasting it."

Jessica nodded, and Karrie watched her walk back toward camp. Todd hadn't emerged from their tent. Seth had disappeared. Rob and Heather were still tête-à-tête from what Karrie could tell.

Her legs were starting to burn and she climbed into the car and sat behind the wheel with her head laid back. She closed her eyes and thought about her conversation with Jessica. Thought about the reporter from the *Review Journal* who was supposed to show up tomorrow.

He was probably going to be ticked off that he drove for two hours and the dig had produced nothing so far. Of course tomorrow was only the fourth day they'd been digging. The journal she'd kept would help. There'd be material to work with so his articles could build to a potential discovery.

She smiled grimly. Ironic, really, that she'd led him to believe Rob was after something, and then got angry when she found out about the Paiute burial site.

The air conditioner couldn't keep up with the outside heat and it was still warm enough in the car to make her drowsy. She kept her eyes closed, thinking about her air-conditioned office in Manhattan. Well, not exactly an office. Yet. What she had was more of a cubicle. But soon…

Amazing, but New York seemed like a million miles away, a totally different era. Had it really been only a week ago that she'd stood out in the rain, cussing under her breath as every cab passed her by?

She missed the window-shopping and street vendors who cooked the best Italian sausage in the world, and the neighborhood pizza that she saved up her calories for each week. But she had to admit, being out here hadn't been half as bad as she expected.

Of course Rob had a lot to do with that. Just thinking about him and last night made her all squishy and warm. Tonight she'd tell him they should share her tent. It was away from everyone else's. They'd just have to be quiet….

The sound of the opening door made her jump. Rob slid into the passenger side.

He smiled and winked. "How about a ride to the river?"

12

"STOP."

Karrie put on the brakes, and they jerked against the seat belts. "What?"

Rob reached for a lock of her ponytail and twirled it around his finger. "You look absolutely beautiful."

"You scared the hell out of me." She put a hand to her throat.

She was the one who scared the hell out of him. He cupped the back of her head and kissed her hard. And long. And thoroughly. He came up for air and said, "I've wanted to do that all day."

"Two more miles and we get to the river. You couldn't wait?" She was trying to hide a pleased smile, but without success.

He grinned. "Ah, sexy and romantic."

She laughed. "Well, you almost gave me a heart attack."

"You're right. That was stupid. I lost my head for a minute."

"I forgive you." She turned her attention back to driving and accelerated again. "But I do expect you to make it up to me."

"Name it."

"Surprise me."

"You giving me carte blanche?"

She wrinkled her perfect little nose. Damn, she was cute. "I have to think about that one."

"You have about five minutes."

"Anxious, are we?"

"Anxious to wipe that smug smile off your face."

She laughed, the seductive sound easing the tightness in his shoulders and back from a morning of hard digging. "We got a late start. How long do we have?"

"As long as we want."

"You know someone will show up soon."

"Yeah." Sighing, he laid his head back. Better than staring at her. Made it too hard to keep his hands off. Last night had been hell. He'd probably slept only a couple of hours. "I was thinking about tonight...."

"You read my mind."

"Your tent or mine?"

"Mine is farther away from Heather." She grimaced. "I meant everybody."

Rob chuckled. "I'm not that stupid. She's been a pain in the ass, but a clever one. She's come up with some legitimate questions I can't ignore."

"Bright girl."

"Yep, self-centered but bright."

"God, I hope I didn't seem like her back in the day."

"Are you kidding? No way. I always thought you were kind of shy."

"I was, really. Living in Manhattan taught me well."

He didn't say anything. He didn't like thinking about her living in New York. Going back there. Inevitable, obviously. But that didn't mean he had to think about it and ruin their last two days.

Realistically, he'd be better off when she left. He'd been too distracted. Not paying enough attention to the students. With the exception of Heather. She was driving him crazy.

"Before we get sidetracked," she said, grinning, "what's the plan for tonight?"

"You're right about your tent. That would be better."

"We just have to wait for everyone to go to sleep."

"You wouldn't happen to have a sleep aid we could put in their dinner?"

She laughed. "You're awful."

"Desperate."

"What am I going to do with you?"

"I have one suggestion."

The tiny dimple at the corner of her mouth flashing, she shook her head. "Who knew?"

"What?"

"Here I thought you were the serious studious type."

"I am."

"Uh-huh."

He reached over to touch her hair. Even pulled back in a ponytail and stuck under the baseball cap it looked good. "Are we there yet?"

She applied the brakes, and he was surprised to see

that they really were there. The Colorado stretched out for miles before them. Cool and inviting. No matter how many times he saw it, the river's untamed beauty always called to his soul, made him feel at peace.

But as much as he loved the outdoors, loved being in the field, right now he wished they were staying at one of the fancy Vegas Strip resorts. With a giant hot tub in the bathroom, a king bed with silk sheets, a bottle of Chardonnay chilling beside the bed. No one around. No planes to catch. No talk of careers and letdowns.

He looked over at her, and she also stared at the river, as if mesmerized by the rushing greenish-blue water taking every curve with fluid grace.

"Beautiful, isn't it?"

Her lips curved slightly. "Yeah, as much as I hate to admit it."

"Why?"

She looked at him. "Why would I hate to admit it?"

He nodded, curious why she resisted this incredible area of the country.

"It's just a figure of speech." She frowned thoughtfully. "No, you're right. I don't know—" She shrugged helplessly. "As a kid I spent so much time thinking up ways to get out that I guess the idea that I hated the place stuck in my head."

"After you left, did you miss it?"

"Nope."

"Really?"

"Believe me, I found no beauty here at all. Especially not in Searchlight." She paused. "It did take me a while to get used to the noise in the city. And the cost of rent. And the trash. Not just littering, but the way they stack trash right on the street for pickup. I know there's no way around it, but eww!"

He smiled. "What do you like about New York?"

Her chin lifted defensively. "Everything else. The restaurants, shopping, the arts, Central Park, the sophistication..."

"Okay, I get it." He reached over and cupped her nape, massaging and kneading until she closed her eyes and let her head drop forward. "We could just stay in the car."

"We could...."

"Or we could risk taking our clothes off and run for the water."

She smiled, her eyes still closed. "I should be giving you a massage. You've been working hard all morning."

"Is that a no on getting naked?"

Laughing, she opened her eyes. "Dr. Philips, what ever happened to all that cautionary discretion?"

He sighed, withdrawing his hand and sitting back to look at her. "Good thing you're leaving in two days."

She blinked, her smile disappearing, hurt clouding her expression.

"That couldn't have come out more wrong if I tried." He urged her toward him and kissed her briefly. "I only meant that I can hardly keep my mind off you."

The hurt eased from her face and she lifted her chin. "Expect me to believe that?"

"Believe this."

He kissed her again, this time more forcefully, coaxing her lips open, and finding her tongue. She gave back, her eagerness fueling him until he cupped a hand under her breast and lowered his head to kiss the tip through her shirt. He felt her nipple tighten, and bit it lightly until she moaned.

She didn't wait for him to ask but pulled her shirt over her head. He freed her breasts and stared at the rosy ripe tips, and then flicked each one with his tongue. She squirmed against his mouth, and then found his arousal, cupping him through his shorts.

He'd gotten hard so fast he feared it wouldn't take much to push him over the edge. Deflecting her, he ran his hand up her inner thigh. Reflexively she squeezed her legs together but too late, he'd reached the promised land.

She was already damp, even through her shorts. He got under the hem, his probing fingers easily navigating the elastic of her panties until he found her slick folds. She moved against him and he slid his finger inside finding her as wet and ready as he was hard.

"Rob," she whispered. "We can't do this. Somebody will—" She whimpered, her body shuddering. "Oh, God, I don't want you to stop, but—"

"Shh. Relax."

"What if someone—"

"We'll hear them."

"I won't."

He smiled. "I will."

Karrie gasped as he slid his finger deeper inside. She couldn't open her eyes. Her lids felt as if they were being weighed down by two boulders. She tried to find his zipper but he wouldn't cooperate. He kept shifting away, working his finger faster and deeper.

"Rob…"

He put his other palm to her cheek, stroking her tenderly. "Come on, baby. I want you to come."

She had no strength left.

She had no defense.

Had no choice.

The explosion started in her head. A second before the first spasm hit. And then it came in waves. Tidal waves. Washing over her and coming again and again before she could pick herself up.

She heard Rob's voice as if in the distance, felt his mouth on hers. Briefly. Too brief. He withdrew his hand and she crashed to the shore.

"Karrie."

She forced her eyes open. Everything seemed hazy.

"Karrie." He repeated her name, his voice stern as he retreated from her altogether. "Karrie, Seth's truck is coming up behind us."

She blinked. Saw that he was holding her shirt out to her. She grabbed it, slumped down and jerked it on.

Rob squeezed her thigh. "They're still several yards back."

She smelled the musky scent of sex and blushed.

"Hey, it's okay," Rob murmured soothingly. "No one saw a thing."

"I don't want to get out of the car."

"Fine. We'll pretend we just got back in. After they get out we'll leave."

She nodded, and looked down to make sure her clothes were in order. Her shorts were still bunched. She quickly tugged the hem down.

Heather was with Seth and she got out of the truck first. Of course she went directly over to Rob's side of the car. She opened the door before either of them could put down the window. Not that Karrie had any intention of doing so.

"Did you guys just get here?" Heather asked Rob, and then slid a look at Karrie.

"Nope. We were actually just leaving."

Heather frowned. "You didn't go swimming? Is it too rough today?" She turned her gaze toward the water, her frown deepening as she looked back at Rob.

"Karrie didn't feel like it."

Heather smiled. "Come with us. We'll drive you back."

Rob shook his head. "Actually, I don't feel like a swim, either. Go ahead."

Seth joined them in time to see Heather purse her lips into a practiced pout. She started to say something, but he grabbed her arm. "Come on," he said as he dragged her with him. "Good thing you're cute because you sure can be a dumb shit sometimes."

Karrie bit her lip to keep from laughing.

Heather stopped, jerked away from him and let fly a healthy curse. Indignantly, she turned back to Rob.

"Heather," he said before she could utter a word. "Go on with Seth. This trip is for you kids, not me. I've got things to do back at camp, and I need to do them with Karrie."

Heather's eyes widened as Rob's words seemed to sink in. She opened her mouth, but Seth tugged her away. "You heard the Professor," Seth said. "Us kids need to take a cold bath."

NO ONE HAD FOUND ANYTHING particularly exciting today so their nightly wrap-up discussion had been short. After dinner, Seth used the table to spread out his star charts and got out his GPS to manually find Saturn and Jupiter. He promised that the rings around Saturn were worth seeing.

Though Karrie wasn't sure he'd have any takers tonight. Rob was busy making notes. Heather was still in a snit from earlier, and Jessica had just led Todd to their tent. For the *talk,* Karrie assumed.

She hoped it went well. She'd feel responsible if it didn't. One of these days maybe she'd learn to keep her big mouth shut.

Sighing, she sank into a chair with her journal on her lap. Today's entries were scarce. Big surprise. Her thoughts had never been far from Rob. Last night. The mesa. His skillful hands...

Damn, she wished he'd hurry with those notes.

Of course she should be making good use of the

time, as well. The reporter was due tomorrow. Which meant her trip was almost over. And tomorrow night would be their last night together.

Her concentration dissolved just like that.

Growling loudly enough that Seth looked away from the sky, Karrie forced her attention back to her journal. Rob was right. It was better that she leave. What bothered her, though, was that he hadn't mentioned anything about seeing each other again. But then neither had she.

It didn't matter. He was only her Man To Do. And man, oh, man, had she done him. Wait till she wrote the gang at Eve's Apple. They'd be so proud....

Her insides tensed. The idea of sharing anything that happened between her and Rob stung. It seemed disloyal—or—just plain wrong. Even if she skipped details.

A strange protective feeling grew inside her, making her uncomfortable, like a dress that was too tight. Damn, what was happening here...

"Hey, Karrie." Seth picked up his charts. "Wanna see something really cool?"

She looked blankly at him.

"Have you ever seen the rings around Saturn?"

She shook her head, her confused thoughts reeling. This was only about sex. Nothing more. She couldn't afford to have feelings for Rob.

"I found it. They call it jewel in the sky because of the rings. We should get a clear shot from out here." He frowned at her. "Are you okay?"

"What? I was just— Yeah, fine."

"Wanna go look?"

Heather walked up in her skimpy shorts, cropped T-shirt with no bra, hands on her hips. "Come on, butthead, I'll go have a look."

A smile tugged at Seth's mouth. "Let's go. If you change your mind, you know where to find us," he said to Karrie before they headed toward his truck at the rear of the camp where they'd set up his telescope.

She watched until they disappeared, and then tried to focus on the journal. She scribbled a couple of entries but her thoughts kept wandering back to Rob, and she glanced at his tent.

With a lantern lit inside, she could make out a partial silhouette. It didn't look as if he was doing much writing. Maybe he was purposely staying away from her. Maybe he felt the same panic that something between them was changing. That wouldn't be totally bad. Unless he was for the status quo and worried that she wanted to change the rules.

Which she didn't. Not really. That would be totally impractical. Of course, they hadn't really talked about expectations....

Abruptly, she stood. She had to stop this craziness in her head. Maybe she ought to go have a look at Saturn. If nothing else, Heather was good for a distraction.

Before Karrie could get away, Jessica emerged from the tent without Todd. She hurried toward Karrie, a smile spreading across her face, and giving a private thumbs-up sign. She glanced over her shoulder, presumably to make sure Todd hadn't followed, and then drew Karrie into the shadows.

"It was awesome," Jessica said too loudly and lowered her voice. "*I* was awesome. I didn't back down once."

Karrie gave her an impulsive hug. "I'm so proud of you."

"Earlier I practiced what I wanted to say and I was really firm about him listening and not interrupting. And he actually did listen. After I was done I thought for sure he'd give me the silent treatment, but he didn't. I swear, I think he even respects me more."

"I wouldn't be surprised. You did good, girlfriend."

"I did, huh?" Jessica beamed. "He says he wants our relationship to work and that things will be different from now on. And if he slips and gets all self-absorbed, he says I have permission to slap him upside the head."

"Wow, you *did* do good."

Jessica giggled and started walking backward. "I'd better get back. I came out to get Cokes."

"I'll see you tomorrow." Karrie shot another look toward Rob's tent. He was still in there, though she couldn't tell what he was doing. It didn't matter. She wasn't going to wait around. Looking through the telescope would probably be fun, anyway.

Heather and Seth were awfully quiet as Karrie approached. In fact, she saw the telescope but didn't see them. The lantern was there, though, lighting the area they had cleared to make the ground flat enough on which to set the tripod.

She was about to call out when she thought she heard something. The noise came from behind a cluster of sage just beyond the light, close to the front of the truck. A rabbit? Or a coyote? She'd heard enough howling the past two nights that it wouldn't surprise her.

About to turn and run, it occurred to her one of the kids might be in trouble. Quietly she inched forward, unsure whether she'd be better off sneaking up or startling the critter. Startling was probably better. Safer, anyway.

She stopped, listened. Stooped to picked up a large rock. Someone moaned, and without another thought she rushed forward ready to hurl her weapon.

Heather, totally naked, was bent over, holding the side of the truck, and moaning as Seth, also naked, entered her from behind. Karrie immediately stepped back and nearly stumbled in her haste to escape.

Seth didn't see her, but Heather did. She blinked in surprise at Karrie, and then closed her eyes and clutched the truck's hood while Seth pumped harder, as if she didn't want to lose the momentum.

Embarrassed, Karrie turned and hurried back to camp, her heart pounding so hard she thought it would explode. How the hell would she be able to face those two later? She almost wished she were leaving tomorrow.

Rob emerged from his tent just as she approached. He smiled. "I feel like a cup of coffee. How about you?"

Heather and Seth? When had that happened? It boggled the mind. "Um, coffee?"

"What's wrong?"

"Nothing." Her mind raced in several directions. She didn't care much for Heather, but she wouldn't say anything to Rob about what she saw. None of her business. "It's too warm for coffee."

Rob's narrowed gaze drifted past her in the direction of the truck. "Were you guys using the telescope?"

"Not me. I think Heather and Seth are. You know what? I think I will have a cup." She busied herself with getting out a pot to put on the fire.

Rob watched her for a few minutes, obviously perplexed by her sudden industriousness. Then he got out a couple of tin cups and came up behind her. "Where are Todd and Jessica?"

"In their tent."

"We're alone?" he whispered, grinning.

She sighed. "For at least a second." Maybe now was a good time for them to sneak into her tent. "I have an idea—"

Heather appeared, fully clothed thank goodness, and purposefully walked toward Karrie and Rob. Karrie mentally cringed.

Rob handed her a cup. "What's your idea?"

"It'll have to wait," she murmured, studying the pot as Heather approached.

"Got it." Rob's gaze went to Heather and he casually drifted away.

Karrie finally looked up when she felt the other woman's gaze. Heather snatched a bottle of water out of the cooler next to Karrie, and leaning close whispered, "Don't worry. It's no big deal. It was just sex."

Karrie managed a smile. "Want some coffee?"

"No, thanks." She uncapped the bottle and tipped it to her lips, and then sauntered off toward her tent, humming an old Doors' song under her breath.

Rob returned with the jar of instant coffee. "I say we get the hell out of here while we still can."

"Where?"

"Your tent."

"But—" Her gaze went to Jessica and Todd's tent. Their lantern had just gone out. "What about Heather and Seth?"

"After this afternoon I don't think they'll bother us."

After what she just saw she had a feeling he was right. She nodded, and they left the coffee and the pot of heated water, and headed for her tent, her pulse quickening with every step.

Mostly because of nerves. Not for fear of discovery. She feared something far worse. Herself. Girls like her and Jessica weren't like Heather. They didn't just have sex. They wanted loyalty, commitment. They wanted to love.

And now was one hell of a time to figure that out.

13

KARRIE SHADED HER EYES and squinted toward the horizon when she thought she saw the bright gleam of sun on metal. She prayed it was the reporter. One-fifteen already. He was late. Probably because she gave him bad directions. Or else someone had removed the red ribbon she'd used to mark the turnoff, which meant the guy would never find the place.

A couple minutes later, a black four-door sedan came into view and crawled toward camp. At least she thought it may have been black once. A good half inch of dust covered the body.

She waved unnecessarily, and he parked the car right behind hers. When he got out he didn't look happy. Standing back to eye his dirty car, he looked even less pleased. Well, she had warned him to use a four-wheel drive. Amazing he made it this far.

"Frank." She approached him and extended her hand after making sure it wasn't too grimy.

"This better be worth it," he grumbled while shaking her hand. "I hadn't realized it was this far off the road. I almost turned around."

"I'm glad you didn't. Come have something to drink."

He unfastened the top two buttons of his white shirt as he walked alongside her toward the canopy. His sleeves had already been rolled up. "You people find anything yet?"

"Dr. Philips will come and brief you. He's reviewing his notes now so he can give you an up-to-date report." She almost did a double take when she spotted Rob crouched near quad three staring at something in his hands. She didn't know what it was but it sure wasn't his notes. Karrie hoped Frank didn't see him and think they were blowing him off.

"You've been out here four days now?" he asked, accepting the bottle of water she handed him.

"Four days, two hours and ten minutes."

He chuckled. "I hear ya. I'm a city guy myself. You're from New York, right?"

"I live in Manhattan." She decided not to mention Searchlight. Although why, she couldn't say.

"I'm from L.A." He had a nice smile. Wavy brown hair. Intense dark eyes. Tall but not too thin. Pretty good-looking, really. Madison would like him. Exactly her type.

"Seriously, it hasn't been too bad out here. I thought I'd die from the heat the first day but I think only because I'd psyched myself up."

He started to look around. "There are six of you out here, right?"

"Right. Have a seat." She gestured to a camp chair that would keep Rob to Frank's back. She tried to not seem obvious but she kept an eye on Rob. He seemed awfully interested in something. Why was he even at quad three? He'd been sitting at the table with his notes just minutes ago.

She smiled at Frank and slid her sunglasses up on her baseball cap. "Two of the students went to the river, and the other two are taking a nap. This is kind of their siesta time since it's the hottest part of the day and they start work at dawn."

"River?" His eyebrows shot up. "The Colorado runs close to here?"

She laughed. "Glad I'm not the only one who didn't know that. Amazing isn't it?"

They made small talk for the next ten minutes and when he started to glance at his watch she brought out the journal she'd kept. She explained how she'd tried to chronicle each phase of the dig, throwing in random thoughts as a lay observer and the excitement and disappointments she herself had felt over each potential discovery.

He seemed impressed and eagerly accepted the notebook, teasing her that he hoped she didn't expect her own byline. At the last moment she realized she didn't want to give up her notes and she thought about asking for the notebook back when he was finished. Just as quickly she decided against it. She'd kept a few pages that had gotten a little too personal. That was enough.

In a few weeks she'd forget all about the experience and end up pitching the notes anyway.

"Would you excuse me," she said ten minutes later when Rob still hadn't shown up. "I'm going to see what's keeping Dr. Philips."

He glanced at his watch again. "Good. I have to get back on the road within an hour to make another appointment in Laughlin."

"No problem." She hurried out toward Rob, who still seemed totally engrossed. Damn it. He knew this was important to her. That she needed to generate as much good publicity as she could for Sanax. She'd explained that if the *Review Journal* got interested enough, maybe the news stations would consider a good little human-interest piece.

When he saw her, he abruptly stood and met her halfway. "Sorry," he muttered. "Lost track of time."

"What were you doing?" She looked past him to the spot where he'd been crouching. He hadn't left anything there, but his hands were empty. "This guy's getting antsy. I don't want him to lose interest in the story."

"I think I can keep him interested." He took her by the elbow and steered her back toward Frank.

Her heartbeat accelerated. "Did you just find something?"

He winked. "Maybe."

She didn't have time to grill him further. Frank had stood and was looking around as he waited for them to approach. She was going to strangle Rob for keeping her in suspense like this.

Karrie promptly made the introductions and the two men shook hands. Frank wasted no time in getting to his questions, and she kept waiting for Rob to say something about what he'd found. He didn't seem in a hurry to volunteer anything but he held Frank's interest.

She watched and listened, her own enthusiasm growing with the obvious passion Rob had for his work. He had an amazing gift for explaining what an archeologist did without allowing his words to sound technical or boring. Made the listener want to get out and dig himself. See what kind of mystery would unfold.

What bothered her was the proprietary pride that had seeped in when she hadn't been on guard. The kind of pride a wife had for her husband. Totally unexpected. Definitely inappropriate. She'd better get that quick.

"What made you select this site, Dr. Philips?" Frank asked as he scribbled notes even though he also used a small tape recorder.

"An old Paiute story that's been passed down through the generations of a massacre along the Colorado. Some people think they buried their dead around here."

"And why would that be of interest to anyone?"

Rob's jaw tensed.

Karrie winced. She gave him a pleading look.

He hesitated, and then said, "The massacre was executed by white cavalry soldiers and hasn't been recorded as historical fact, we think, because the government at the time was embarrassed after having just signed a treaty."

Frank nodded, his eyes on his notes as he scribbled. But he didn't seem especially impressed.

"I don't know how long you've lived in the area, Frank, but we have a significant Paiute population in Southern Nevada. Many of those massacred were these people's ancestors. I think they may want to know where and how they were buried."

Frank looked up and met his eyes. "You know a Paiute who has a personal interest in this? That would make a great angle for the story."

Rob blinked. "Let's see if what we found amounts to anything first."

Karrie kept quiet. Nothing would make her urge him to discuss his sick friend. Not even the promise of a front page story. Of course that might make her think twice...

Frank straightened, his interest clearly piqued. "So you have found something?"

Rob nodded. "Human bones."

Stunned, Karrie stared at him. She hadn't heard. Was that what he'd been looking at?

"A lot?"

"I don't know. We have to excavate further." Rob's noncommittal answer was met with a brief silence.

And then Frank's eyebrows drew together in a skeptical frown. "Granted, finding human bones way out here does seem unusual, but that in itself wouldn't indicate a burial ground."

"I agree." He hesitated. "But we also found bones

that look as if they belong to a horse. It was common for the dead to be buried with their animals."

Karrie gaped at him. Was this for real? Or was he trying to boost Frank's interest? If that's what it was, the ploy was working. The reporter quickly scribbled more notes, his fascination clearly growing.

"What else?" he asked without looking up.

Rob smiled wryly. He didn't like being put in the hot seat, but he was a PR person's dream. Smooth. Knowledgeable. Professional yet charming. Karrie didn't know if she should be grateful for the snow job, or really pissed off that he'd been holding back.

"There may be possible traces of rabbit fur," he said finally. "The Indians used to make blankets out of the strips of skin."

"Which they would have used to wrap their dead," Frank said absently, as if already writing the story in his head. "When will you be able to confirm any of this?"

"We still have a lot of excavation ahead of us."

Karrie had forced herself to sit quietly until now. "Sounds like two stories to me. One now, indicating what the dig has produced so far and what's speculated, and then a follow-up later after…"

At Frank's pointedly annoyed look, she shut up. It wasn't as if she was telling him how to do his job. She'd only been trying to help.

"I have a question for you," he said, regarding her closely. "What's in it for—" He glanced at his notes. "Sanax?"

"Well, nothing."

He laughed. "Hard to believe."

"I agree," Rob cut in. "But the truth is, I asked and they graciously granted access to the property."

Frank turned back to Karrie. "What does Sanax have planned for the land?"

"Nothing so far. It was bought on spec back in the early sixties," she answered patiently, although she'd already covered this with him after she issued the press release and schmoozed him into writing the article.

"And if it's determined that this is a Paiute burial ground, how will that affect Sanax?" Frank asked, his pen poised.

Silently she cleared her throat. She didn't like the question. Hated answering. Loathed the idea of him quoting her. "I don't see that it will."

He narrowed his gaze, assessing her, probably wondering if she were that naive or simply wanted to dodge the question. "You know, of course, that if this is in fact burial ground the government will get involved. If I'm not mistaken, they'd have the option of seizing the land, wouldn't they?"

"This is just a small parcel. Sanax owns a hundred acres of land in this area."

"Yes, but I would think everything would be frozen until evaluations are made as to how much of the land contains remains." He looked at Rob. "Am I right?"

Rob's eyes stayed on Karrie, and he slowly nodded.

She took a deep breath. "I really can't speak for my company on a matter we haven't yet encountered," she said carefully. "I will say something off-the-record." She waited for Frank to nod and then continued, "If anything is confirmed, I believe Sanax would be supportive of Dr. Philips' efforts. I wouldn't be surprised if they bestowed the land as a gift to the University."

Rob's gaze bored into her. He didn't look happy. So what was up with that?

Frank grinned. "You sure you want this off-the-record?"

She gave him a murderous look. It's not that she didn't believe her own press. The more she thought about it, the more the notion made sense. Giving the useless land as a gift would get incredible publicity and be a terrific tax write-off.

Frank looked at his watch again. "I have to leave. But I want to take a few pictures first."

"Fine," Rob said, immediately standing. "But I can't let you get too close to the quads—" He gestured. "Where we're actually excavating. I don't want the ground disturbed."

"I understand." He got to his feet and pulled a small digital camera out of his pocket. "Karrie, when are you headed back to Las Vegas?"

"Tomorrow."

"If I have any questions, I'll call."

"I leave for New York at six-fifteen." She rose. "But you have my cell number."

"Yeah, I do. Good." He stuck out his hand. "Thanks for your time. Both of you."

Rob accepted his handshake, excused himself and then headed back to quad four.

Karrie stayed with Frank while he took a few snapshots. As she walked him back to his car, she said, "I don't suppose you want to show me the article before it goes to press."

Laughing, he got in the car. "Nice try."

She smiled, shrugged and stepped away from the vehicle. "Have a safe trip home."

After he'd turned around and was headed toward the highway, she walked back toward Rob. He saw her and met her partway.

She shook her head. "I am so mad at you."

"Why?"

She stared in disbelief. "When were you going to tell me about the find?"

"Look." He put up a hand. "I found the bones just before we knocked off for lunch. The rest of the gang don't even know yet."

"Before lunch." That hurt.

"I know for sure there are human bones. I think we have horse bones, as well. But to be honest, I shouldn't have said so much. I wanted you to get your article so I made the situation sound better than it looks."

"I don't buy it." She hadn't meant to say that out loud. Too late. "I'm flattered that you wanted to help me out but you're too much of a professional to allow a report on a dig you're heading to be misrepresented."

He grunted. "What about you? Sticking your neck out like you did. What the hell were you thinking?"

She didn't have to ask what he meant. Obviously she hadn't been thinking when she implied Sanax would be okay with a major find, and that they might even gift the land to UNLV. That would be her recommendation, because she still believed that was the best course of action, but she'd spoken prematurely. And to a reporter. She'd didn't even want to think about it.

"Can I see what you've found?"

"Not yet."

"What?" She'd obviously misheard.

"Here comes Seth and Heather."

She glanced over her shoulder to see the truck coming. Or at least the dust from the truck.

"Look, I don't want to say anything about the bones to the others yet."

"You're kidding." When he didn't answer, she asked, "Why not?"

"No sense them getting disappointed if I'm wrong."

"They're not children. This is all part of the experience." She stared at the strong pulse at his neck. His jaw was clenched. "What's going on? You should be ecstatic, but you're acting weird."

He drew in a long deep breath and then exhaled slowly. Sunglasses protected his eyes. She wanted to take them off. See if his eyes provided any clues. Something was wrong. And he was shutting her out. She hated it, but what right did she have to make demands?

Rob touched her arm, lightly caressed the skin inside her wrist. "We'll talk about it later, okay? Just go with me on this."

"Of course. They're your students." She hadn't meant to sound abrupt. "I don't want to ruin our last night together."

His weary sigh gave her some satisfaction. "What time will you leave tomorrow?"

"In the morning. No sense in me hanging around while you're working." She paused. "You know, it's almost the weekend, sort of. I suppose I could delay my flight. That would give me a few more—"

He'd already started shaking his head. "No, I think it's best you go tomorrow."

She was sure he was right. She knew she messed with his concentration. It still hurt, though.

He smiled. "How about we plan on meeting in three or four weeks when I'm finished here? Can you get some time off? I can go to New York. Or we can meet somewhere in between. Your choice."

Her heart somersaulted. They hadn't once spoken of the future. "I'd like that."

"I'm looking forward to it already."

"You think you'll be out of here in three weeks?"

"Yeah. Seth and one of the others start summer-school classes."

"But what if you really have found something? Won't that change everything?"

He stopped touching her. He lowered his hand to his side, looking hesitant, almost sad. "It will."

"But that would be good, right?" Something inside her twisted with alarm. For them, it simply meant she'd come here or they'd meet later.

"Right," he agreed quietly.

So why didn't she believe him?

14

THE EVENINGS USUALLY dragged by. Tonight had to be the absolute worst. On the one hand, Karrie was glad because it drew out her last night with Rob. But she couldn't wait for everyone to go to their damn tents so she and Rob could go to hers.

It was silly, really. To be acting like children hiding from their parents. Especially since the kids had to know about them. At least Seth and Heather knew. And Jessica probably. Karrie sighed. Oh, brother, who were they kidding?

She'd started a new notebook, this one more personal, and she looked up from her latest entry and slid Rob a sidelong glance. Totally preoccupied with his own notes, he didn't notice.

Jessica did, though. She'd just put away the dinner things and she stared openly at Karrie, her eyes way too knowing.

Karrie went back to writing feverishly in her notebook, wondering what else Jessica had seen. Like how distant Rob had been all evening. Not just with Karrie but with everyone. But of course she took it personally.

If he hadn't seemed so sincere about meeting at a later date, she would have figured he was blowing her off.

He was simply preoccupied. That's all. Nothing to fret over. It would be okay once they were alone. In her tent. Making love.

If everyone would just get the hell to bed.

Abruptly, she stood and stretched.

Rob looked up, his expression blank. "What time is it?" he asked at the same time he glanced at his watch and frowned. "Where is everyone?"

"Heather and Seth are using the telescope." *Yeah, right.* But she kept that to herself. "I'm not sure where Todd is."

"He's in our tent reading," Jessica said. "I'm headed there now. We're turning in early."

Karrie didn't miss the smile in the other woman's voice. She didn't know if that meant "turning in" was a euphemism for "the sex has been great since we talked" or "the coast is clear you guys go ahead and have at it."

Of course since Karrie tended to think everything was about her, Jessica had meant the latter.

"I'm making some coffee," she said. "Anyone else?"

"Sure. I'll take some," Rob murmured, his head already bent, his gaze on his notes, looking like the proverbial absentminded professor.

"Not for me, thanks." Jessica darted Rob a look and motioned for Karrie to follow her, and then headed into the shadows behind the supply tent.

Curious, Karrie joined her. She hoped everything

was okay with her and Todd. They seemed to be getting along great. But Karrie knew how deceiving appearances could be.

"What's up?" she asked, careful to keep her voice down.

Jessica hesitated, nervously tucking her hair behind her ear. "I know you didn't ask, and I know it's none of my business but— Ohhh—" She groaned. "Don't hate me."

"What?" Karrie tried not to yell. "Just spit it out."

"I think you should follow the same advice you gave me," Jessica said in a rush.

"That being?"

"Talk to him."

Karrie folded her arms across her chest. "This is different." She sighed. "Does everyone know?"

Jessica nodded, shrugged. "It's kind of obvious... you know. The way he looks at you and all."

"Not tonight," Karrie muttered, somewhat pacified that he'd at least been looking at some point.

"That's what I mean. Did you guys have a fight?"

"No, he's just busy."

"Then why are you so upset?"

Karrie let her arms fall to her sides. "I hate leaving tomorrow." That was half-true.

"Oh. That." Jessica smiled. "I'm glad you didn't split up or anything. You guys are perfect together."

"Yeah." Karrie laughed.

Jessica frowned with uncertainty. As if she didn't

know what that meant but she wasn't saying anything more. "Sorry I butted in."

"No problem. We all need reminders." Karrie good-naturedly shouldered her arm, and then started them back. "Go spend time with Todd. Quit worrying about me."

"Okay. 'Night." She smiled, and then turned in the direction of her tent.

Karrie went back to making coffee. Rob didn't even look up. Probably hadn't even realized she was gone. Maybe Jessica was right. Maybe they did need to have a talk. Maybe he'd suggested they meet later out of a sense of obligation because she'd gone to bat for him. If that was it, she didn't need his gratitude. Certainly didn't want it.

She was going to drive herself crazy. Looks as if they did have to talk. Whatever the outcome, she could handle it. No problem.

She dropped a spoon and it bounced off the cast-iron pot, making a loud clattering sound. Rob looked up, his lips curving.

He laid down his pen. "Trying to tell me the coffee's ready?"

"Yep. And it worked."

His smile faded. "I've neglected you tonight. I'm sorry."

"I was joking." She brought him a cup of strong dark coffee, sugar, no cream. All they had was the powdered stuff which tasted nasty. She didn't use it, either. "I know you have to work."

"But it's your last night." He accepted the tin cup and

then held it up as if in salute. "Thank you. Not just for this. You've been a great sport. You've done much more around here than you should have."

That was the perfect opening. She took a deep breath. "I've enjoyed being included. You don't need to thank me." She held up a hand when he started to interrupt. "About meeting later in the summer…I know you're going to be busy and…"

His face fell.

She'd started out wrong. "The thing is, I don't want you to feel— Look, we didn't make any promises to each other, okay? And if you—"

"Karrie?" His unwavering gaze met her squarely in the eyes.

"What?"

His expression completely unreadable, he quietly asked, "Are you trying to tell me to take a hike?"

Stunned, she opened her mouth but nothing came out.

"Yes or no."

"No. Not even close. I was trying to let you off the hook."

A smile slowly curved his mouth and lit up his face. He put down the coffee, closed his notebook and stood. Holding out his hand to her he said, "Come on."

She quickly glanced around.

However he didn't seem to care if anyone could see them.

"Where are we going?" she asked as she took his hand, her pulse suddenly erratic.

"To show you exactly where I want to be." He pulled her closer and led her to the tent.

HE HELD OPEN THE FLAP TO HER, and as she ducked in, she was struck again by just how small the space was. Tiny. They'd have to be scrunched together in order to do this thing, which was okay with her.

Ever since he'd put his arm around her, she'd been all fluttery. Her stomach, her pulse, her breath. He stepped inside and immediately zipped the tent, giving them privacy. The only light came from the lantern in the far corner. Her pack was perched against the tent next to the light, and on the ground was her sleeping bag.

Rob looked at her, then at the ground. Instead of taking her in his arms, he knelt, spreading the bag completely open, making a soft, well, relatively soft, bed for the two of them. Then he stood again, his smile warming her from the inside out.

"Do something for me?"

She nodded. Anything he wanted was fine by her.

"Take off your clothes."

Her face immediately heated. It's not as if he hadn't seen her naked, but she wasn't exactly the striptease type.

He looked at her with such hunger, such appreciation, that her embarrassment eased. Especially when he lifted his T-shirt off in one fluid movement, leaving his incredible chest bare. The way the light shone, he was mostly in shadow. She was fully lit, so he'd see everything. Her curves, her flaws, the scar on her left hip. Which didn't seem to matter in the least.

She took off her top, so she stood before him in her sport bra and shorts. His sigh made her grin as she hooked her fingers underneath the waistband of her shorts. Taking her time, she slid the material down, leaving her panties on.

Her gaze moved to his as her shorts puddled at her feet. He seemed enraptured by the view. His eyes wide, his smile broad, he looked her up and down slowly, lingering where parts were still hidden.

"Oh, God," he said.

She concurred.

He unzipped his shorts and dropped them, along with his boxers, revealing his enthusiasm in the most graphic way. He didn't seem impressed, but she certainly was. In fact, it was a little difficult to think or look at anything else.

"More," he whispered.

"I can't see how," she said. "I mean, wow."

He laughed. "Not me. You."

"Oh." She giggled as she slipped her sport bra up and off.

"Lovely," Rob said, still standing too far away.

She didn't like the separation, so she slid off her panties with no more fanfare. Well, maybe that one little swish of her hips.

He was next to her in a heartbeat, but instead of touching any of the obvious parts, his hands went to her face, cupping her cheeks. "Thank you," he said, as if she'd given him the only thing he'd ever wanted.

"My pleasure."

"Not yet, but soon," he said. And then he pulled her into a kiss that made her knees weak. His talented tongue did wicked things that she could only trace, teasing and diving and sweeping. Her hands went to his shoulders, holding on for dear life as she could no longer balance on her own.

He was the one to pull back, leaving her gasping. When he stepped back, she tried to stay close, but he had other ideas. "Lay down," he said.

That seemed a very good idea, and she did, as delicately as she could, which wasn't easy, considering. But finally, she was atop the sleeping blanket and he stood over her, breathing hard...which wasn't the only part of him hard.

He turned to the side, ready to join her, but in that moment, his shadow loomed large on the side of the tent, with one particular attribute jutting out like a lance.

Karrie couldn't help but laugh. She just hoped all the kids were safely in their tents, or they'd be getting a brand-new picture of their beloved professor.

His eyebrows went down. "What?"

She couldn't speak yet, but she could point. He turned, saw the shadow and the interesting proportions and dived to the sleeping bag. He looked horrified, mouth open, eyes panicked as he grabbed the lantern and struggled to turn it off.

The darkness came over them like a blanket, and

she struggled to stifle her giggles, but then she heard his soft laughter, and felt his hand run over the curve of her hip, and everything was okay. Better than okay.

"Come here, you goof," he said, tugging her close.

"You have to admit, it was one hell of a puppet show."

"Too bad it doesn't do tricks."

"I don't know about that," she said. "I'm thinking it's pretty damn talented." Her hand moved around his length, grateful the impromptu shadow dance hadn't diminished him in the least.

"It has nothing to do with talent," Rob said. "I just know where I want to be. The best place on earth."

"Oh, gosh."

He laughed again. "You sound like a kid."

She rubbed her chest against his. "I don't feel like one."

"No, indeed you don't," he whispered, his voice lower, gruffer and full of need.

"I can't believe this is our last night."

His finger came to her lips. "Shh. We won't talk about that, now. Tonight is endless. And all ours. No tomorrow. Nothing but you and me."

She opened her mouth, but her words were lost in a kiss. Languid, bittersweet, he took his time, and she took hers, exploring, memorizing.

His hands roamed her body, touching her everywhere, as gentle as a whisper and oh, so tender. She gave herself permission to do the same, and she found his chest, that hard chiseled marble encased in soft skin, the silky texture of his hair irresistible to her seeking fingers.

His leg maneuvered between hers, and his thigh pressed her core tightly, making her moan. She wriggled against him, aching for the friction she needed like air.

His hard cock pressed between them, his maleness making her feel soft and vulnerable. Everything about his body contrasted with hers in the most incredible way, and she simply couldn't get enough.

His lips left hers only to find the hollow of her neck. She sighed, loving the way he licked and tasted her, as if she was the sweetest treat. But now she wanted more.

She pulled back, and gripping his shoulders, maneuvered him onto his back. She smiled, knowing he couldn't see her, and gave him a brief kiss on the lips. Then she climbed over him, and moved down until she could take his hard nipple between her lips.

He gasped as she flicked her tongue over the small bead. Inarticulate words floated over her head as she sucked and nibbled until it was time to give equal treatment to the other side of his chest.

His hands were in her hair, petting, restrained. She wondered if he'd be so tender when she moved down, licking his body in a wet stream as she inched lower and lower until finally she had him just where she wanted him. Grasping his thickness with one hand, she pulled back her hair with the other so that nothing would get in the way. Then she licked his tip. Once. Twice. Three times.

"Karrie!" he said, as his upper body arched off the sleeping bag.

"Shh," she said. "Relax."

"Are you joking?"

She didn't answer him. She was too busy. He was thick and hot and it made her shiver to learn him this way. Licking up and down, taking him as far as she could into her mouth, flicking with her tongue, she was driving him crazy and that was as luscious as her own response.

He moaned rather loudly. It was a good thing the students were probably too busy with their own shenanigans to care. Because she wasn't about to hold back. Not that she could.

"Wait," he said, in more of a gasp than a word.

He sat up, dislodging her. With stunning strength he pulled her forward, kissing her hotly, desperately. He broke away, found his pants and prepared himself while she counted her heartbeats.

Then she was straddling him once again, and his lips found hers for another astonishing kiss. Without breaking the kiss, she rose on her knees, held him steady, then lowered herself ever so slowly. Inch by thick inch, until he filled her completely.

He moaned again, and she pushed him gently back until he was lying down. Then she rode him. Taking her time, positioning herself so that every time she moved, she rubbed herself perfectly. Time stopped, the earth stopped, but her pace quickened as the tension inside her built. She threw her head back, eyes closed, focusing on the sensations rippling through her body.

He bucked, thrust, and when she was almost there,

he lifted the both of them until it was her on the bottom, with her legs crossed over his back, and it was him setting the pace, driving her wild, taking her to the edge.

She screamed when it hit, but his mouth covered hers and swallowed her passion, her intensity. She came, so hard she almost passed out, and then he stiffened, cried out, and she held him as he trembled and shook.

Finally, he relaxed, lowered himself to her side. Their panting breaths filled the small tent as she wallowed in her amazing sense of completion. When his hand moved gently to her tummy, hot tears burned her eyes. She wasn't sure which was more powerful. How incredible it was to have shared this moment, or how sad it was that it was possibly the only moment they'd have.

ROB FINISHED LOADING Karrie's car. Along with her own stuff she'd offered to take back their bags of trash, plastic bottles and tin cans to recycle and anything else they didn't need. He'd left her tent up for now. That, he'd worry about later.

Shading his eyes, he scanned the camp and saw her talking to Jessica near the supply tent. The sun glinted off her auburn hair, pulled back into a messy ponytail. Her arms and long tempting legs weren't so pale anymore, but slightly golden and entirely too distracting.

Good thing she was leaving. Except, damn it, he missed her already. He'd miss her quick wit, her willingness to help at every turn. He'd miss her ready smile. He'd damn well miss her generosity in bed.

Just thinking about last night got him hard and he sauntered off toward the site so he could loosen his shorts. It wasn't just the sex that had him reeling. That part was great. The best he'd ever had.

But something about Karrie reached in and touched his soul, captured his heart as no one or nothing else could. The feeling was almost mystical. This whole co-incidence of her showing up as the Sanax rep was the damnedest thing. As if fate realized he'd been cheated before and brought her back into his life when they were both older, wiser to give them a second chance.

He stopped short of quad four and stared at the area he'd roped off and covered with a tarp to hide the blu-ish-gray dirt he couldn't allow her to see. He tossed a guilty look over his shoulder.

She'd left the others and was walking toward him, her car keys in her hand. He turned to meet her halfway.

God help him, but he hoped he wasn't about to blow it. Because fate, with its fickle sense of humor, hadn't made it easy. The second chance came with a built-in obstacle. A test. And time alone would tell if he'd pass and win Karrie. Or lose her forever.

15

I'm sitting in McCarran airport waiting for my flight back to New York. I had to write. Couldn't wait another minute. I'm tired, achy, sunburned, mildly dehydrated, my hair sucks and my lips are unspeakably chapped and I possibly have screwed myself out of a promotion.

That said, I had the most amazing five days!!!

I hate that it's ended. Really.

I'll get to the good stuff. Rob (my MTD of course) is everything I thought he'd be. That whole fantasy thing can be tricky. I had this well-crafted image in my head, and at the tender age of twenty when I was much more worldly ☺, of how perfect he was. Charming, smart, fabulous sense of humor, great bod, a sexual Zeus, a guy who actually *talks*... Guess what? He's everything and more!

It's not over, either. We're meeting again in a month

or so. Somewhere in between coasts. The only problem is me trying to concentrate on work until then. The good news is he's incommunicado being out in the desert for the next two weeks, so long, all-hours-of-the-night phone calls won't be a distraction. The bad news is he's incommunicado. It's gonna drive me nuts not hearing from him.

Oh, well. Life goes on.

Gotta go. They just called for my flight to board. I'll write more later. Hope you guys are all doing well. Be good. Be safe. Have lots of fun.

Karrie

SHE CLOSED HER LAPTOP and slumped in her chair. She wasn't getting up until the last call to board. Flying didn't bother her. Being stuck on a plane next to a stranger and sitting on the ground waiting was what made her crazy.

She wanted to close her eyes, but she didn't dare. A few seconds of total relaxation and for sure she'd miss her flight. She was really that tired. Especially after last night...

Oh, God, she couldn't think about last night. Or Rob. Or how she hated the thought of not seeing him for a month. She'd kept the e-mail breezy, joked about losing her promotion because the feelings building inside were too overwhelming to analyze, much less share.

Could she really have fallen in love with him so quickly? Exhaustion made her emotional and she was really going to have to be careful. The separation was good. Really. It would give her time to think. Get back into her job, her friends, her old routine.

Her eyes started to drift closed and she forced them open.

Of course, missing her flight wouldn't be all bad. She didn't have to be in the office until Monday. She could drive back to the site. Just for one more day. She still believed a healthy separation wouldn't hurt. Eventually.

The agent announced the last boarding call.

Sighing, Karrie pushed to her feet. It all seemed so damn anticlimactic. The whole trip. Not just with Rob. But she had to admit, she'd gotten pretty caught up in the excitement of the dig. Waking up each day wondering what might be unearthed. Heck, just watching the others get excited had been exciting.

And now that there seemed to be a payoff, she was missing out.

Yeah, she'd gotten to see the bones in question. Watched Rob use a small artist's paintbrush to delicately brush away dirt and sand. Never would she have guessed that staring at brittle old faded bones would bring a lump to her throat and make her heart race. It was really something. Indescribable, really.

No one else stood at the gate, and the boarding agent looked pointedly at Karrie. She hefted her carry-on and moved forward. Life in New York awaited.

THE SOHO BAR WAS PACKED with an after-work crowd mixed with yuppies and Bohemian types in monochro-

matic black that included lipstick and nail polish. The
eclectic clientele and decor made it one of Karrie's fa-
vorites. She'd lived in New York City for two years before she'd learned not to gape.

She'd arrived early and ordered a peach martini
while she waited for Madison. Normally, Karrie
wouldn't have left the office before six-thirty, especially after being back for only three days. But she'd
been restless today. On a scale of one-to-ten, her abil-
ity to concentrate—minus two.

Not totally true. When she thought about Rob, her
concentration was perfect. She recalled every inch of his
chest, the crisp softness of his chest hair beneath her fingers. The ridges of muscle down his belly. His eager
mouth suckling her nipples…how he knew just how to
touch her…how much pressure to use…

She took a quick sip of her martini, and then shifted
in her seat. Getting damp, for goodness' sakes. This was
not good. Not good at all.

"Hey."

She looked up, glad to see Madison, who'd been out
of town. They hadn't talked yet. Only e-mailed. "Hey."

"I thought I'd beat you here."

"I left the office at six."

Dressed in jeans, a white T-shirt and blue blazer,
Madison slid into the small booth. "I almost didn't see
you. Why aren't you sitting at the bar?"

Karrie shrugged. "I didn't feel like making small
talk with anyone."

"Ah." She nodded at Karrie's martini. "You didn't happen to order me one of those."

"I did. Peach, like mine."

"You're the best." She tilted her head to the side. "You look great."

"You like the peeling-nose look?"

Madison peered closer and laughed. "Don't worry. You did a good job of covering it up. Seriously. The suntan, outdoorsy look agrees with you."

Karrie sighed. "I do miss getting up in the morning and pulling on shorts instead of a suit and panty hose."

"Yeah, I couldn't do the suit thing." She plucked at her T-shirt. "One of the perks of a freelance photographer."

"When did you get back? Last night or this morning?"

"Last night. I just came from a shoot."

The waitress brought Madison's drink. While her friend ordered munchies, Karrie thought about the Armani suit she'd been saving up for. Obscenely expensive, she'd justified setting aside some money for it out of last year's generous bonus. Funny, but right now she could barely remember what it looked like.

"Okay." After her first sip, Madison put down her martini. "Tell me everything."

Karrie laughed. "No foreplay?"

"No. Now."

"Okay, then." Karrie took a breath. "I know you won't believe this but—everything that Madam Zora predicted happened."

"Everything?" Madison slathered the word with skepticism like butter on bread.

She nodded. "Seriously."

Her friend pursed her lips thoughtfully. "I have to admit, after her saying there'd be someone from your past and then you suddenly going back to Vegas and seeing your old professor…well, that is totally unreal. Freaked me out."

"Well, yeah. Not to mention everything else that happened just like she predicted."

"Okay, details."

Karrie cleared her throat.

Madison leaned forward, her eyes widening. "Are you blushing? Oh, my, God, you're blushing."

"Could you get a little louder? I don't think they heard you in Queens."

"Sorry." Madison pressed her lips together, and glanced at the bearded guy sitting at the bar watching them. "Tell me everything."

"I'll tell you what, kiddo. You'd better be afraid. Very afraid. If my prediction came true then…"

Madison paled. "I have never gotten involved with a client in my life. Never will. Besides, I've got this Man of the Month project that'll keep me plenty busy."

Karrie really shouldn't have taken pleasure in her friend's panic-stricken look. She grinned. "Maybe that's the guy the psychic said you were going to have that wild passionate fling with."

"Don't even joke about that." Madison shuddered

and grabbed her martini. "Anyway, we're talking about you."

Karrie quickly sobered, and paused to take a deep fortifying breath. "I think I'm in trouble."

The glass froze halfway to Madison's lips. She slowly put the martini back on the table. "It's serious?"

"It could be. Oh, God, Madison, he's so perfect. I mean it. I can't think of a single thing I'd change about him. Not a one. Nada."

"Oh, I think him living over two thousand miles away might be a minor point to take into account."

"You know what I mean."

Madison gave her an apologetic smile. "Are you considering a long-distance relationship?"

"We've talked about meeting halfway in between in a month or so, but I think discussing anything long-term would be premature." She'd thought about little else. Dissected her calendar trying to figure out how she could squeeze in extra days around long weekends. For the first time in five years, she wasn't planning her life around her career.

It was scarier than hell. Deliriously exciting. She hoped she wasn't being a total fool.

"For him or you?"

Karrie sighed. "I don't know. Honestly. Things happened quickly."

Silence stretched between them for a few moments. Finally, Madison's lips curved in a teasing grin. "The sex was that good, huh?"

Karrie just smiled.

Madison stared at her for a moment, concern in her eyes, then slumped back and picked up her martini. "She ain't talking. It's got to be serious."

HER OVERFLOWING IN-BOX toppled to the floor at the same time her phone rang for the third time in five minutes. Karrie muttered a curse and grabbed the receiver.

"Karrie Albright." With the toe of her black heel she tried to move the folder of last year's Macy's Thanksgiving Day parade pictures toward her.

"Hey, it's Madison. You want to meet for a drink after work?"

"Sorry. Can't. I have a deadline tomorrow."

"No problem. I'm headed to Chicago in the morning. I'll call you when I get back."

"I'll try to be caught up by then." She laughed without humor and they hung up.

At least that hadn't been another call from marketing or legal asking her for something she'd promised them a week ago. The unexpected Las Vegas trip had really put her behind. But the excuse could only go so far. She'd been back an entire week and had spent far too much time daydreaming about Rob. She'd also spent a considerable amount of time putting together a proposal to present to Sandhill.

She'd tried her best to remain unbiased and she still thought Sanax's best course of action would be to donate the land to the university. The move certainly wouldn't hurt her career, either. She'd have taken a worthless piece of land and parlayed it into a publicist's dream.

So far, Sandhill was pleased with the amount of publicity she'd generated. Her report to him had been brief. The *Review Journal* was publishing a series of articles in the Sunday paper for the next four weeks with Sanax's name prominently mentioned.

He hadn't asked for copies, only told her to retain them in the file. Good thing. She hadn't advised him of the burial ground possibility yet. Better to have a total report and recommendation put together, she'd decided.

She'd gotten most of the file folders picked up off the floor when Kelly, one of the admin assistants, poked her head into Karrie's cubicle.

"You got a minute?" the blonde asked. Today her hair was spiked with pink highlights.

"Only one."

"You're gonna kill me but I screwed up one of your letters." She made a face as she handed Karrie a sheet of paper. "The one you wanted like yesterday. You'll have to proof it and then I'll retype it. I think you need a new Dictaphone. Too much static."

Karrie sighed. Could anything else go wrong today? "Thanks, Kelly. I'll get it right back to you."

"Okay. Whenever." Kelly left, but in two seconds she was back. "I almost forgot. Mr. Sandhill wants you in his office immediately." She glanced down the hall and in a lowered voice added, "He looked really pissed."

Karrie groaned. "Thanks."

Butterflies started in her tummy and she put the letter aside, instantly forgotten. The summons could only be about one thing. She generally didn't have dealings with Sandhill. Only regarding the Nevada land.

She stopped briefly in the ladies' rest room. Made sure her hair was neatly pulled back. Adjusted her skirt. Tucked in her blouse where it had pulled from her waistband.

After waiting for what seemed like an hour for the elevator, Karrie took it to Sandhill's office two floors up. She'd worked herself into a pretty good panic by the time she knocked on his door. His barked, "come in," didn't help.

She closed the door behind her and smiled. "Good morning, Mr. Sandhill. You wanted to see me?"

His face stern, his bushy eyebrows drawn into one furry line giving him a fierce look, he stared at her long enough for her stomach to do several flip-flops. "Is there something you wanted to tell me?"

Asking for a clue would probably tick him off. She cleared her throat. "I assume you're talking about the Nevada situation?"

Clasping his hands behind his head, he leaned back in his chair and regarded her with ill-concealed irritation. He hadn't asked her to sit, so she continued to stand across the massive desk from him.

She really had no idea what this was about. Maybe he'd finally read one of the reporter's articles citing the hope was that a burial ground would be found. If he had, she had only herself to blame for withholding information from him. She still felt she'd handled the situation correctly, though. Waiting until her proposal was complete before giving him details.

Finally, he unclasped his hands and leaned forward. In front of him was a sheet of paper he slid across the desk toward her. "Explain this."

She immediately recognized the State of Nevada letterhead. Without an invitation, she sank into a chair, and willed her hands not to shake as she picked up the letter.

Quickly, she read it to herself. Her heart sank with each sentence. Funny how two short paragraphs could torpedo her entire career.

The State of Nevada, in accordance with the terms of the initial purchase agreement, had frozen the land until a determination had been made regarding the existence of a Paiute burial ground.

She sank back, stunned.

"Well?" Sandhill tapped a finger on his desk. The only sound in an otherwise silent abyss.

It had been only nine days since she'd left Nevada. Since she'd seen Rob.

The son of a bitch knew.

Karrie drew in a deep breath. She couldn't think about him right now. She needed all her wits about her. "Actually," she said calmly, "I knew finding a burial ground was a possibility. In fact, it was the carrot I dan-

gled in front of the reporter in order to get the coverage
we received. Otherwise, there really was no hook."

Sandhill's frown deepened, but he said nothing.

"Frankly, I think this is excellent news. The land is
useless." She gave him her best smile. "Or should I say
was useless. We'll get a lot of good press out of this.
Look like real philanthropists. The environmentalists
will be happy, as will the Indian rights' activists. I think
it's a win-win situation."

Sandhill took back the letter and silently read it
again. When he was through, he leaned back, looking
considerably less angry. But not totally convinced, either. "Be that as it may, I don't like surprises."

"Yes, sir, I understand." Did she ever. Her anger
hadn't as easily subsided. Rob had had time to contact
the State but not her? If the evidence wasn't before her,
she wouldn't have believed it.

Not Rob. But here it was. In black and white.

Damn him.

She struggled to maintain her composure as anger
mushroomed into hurt. Anger was by far preferable. But
she had to ignore her personal feelings. She wasn't in
the clear yet. Damage control. That had to be her focus.
She breathed in deeply.

"To be honest," she said slowly, "I've been working
on a proposal that I feel would net us maximum benefit. I wanted to do more study before I submitted it for
your consideration, but in the circumstances, I'd like to
give you a sketch."

He nodded, and she continued. "Since we currently have no use for the land and it's highly unlikely we could sell it, I believe donating it to the university might be to our advantage."

His face lit with interest and she went on to explain the tax write-off value in addition to the publicity she felt she could milk from the donation. He allowed her to go into significant detail without interrupting which she took as a good sign.

Finally, he said, "I like it."

Relief engulfed her. "I'll work on a press release right away."

"No. First you're getting on a plane to Vegas. Tonight."

16

KARRIE HADN'T PACKED MUCH. Didn't need it. How long would it take to find out why Rob had screwed her over? She gripped the steering wheel tighter, reminded herself she needed to concentrate on her driving. Finding the turnoff was tricky enough. Trying to find it through a river of tears wouldn't help.

Actually, so far she hadn't shed a single one. Partly because she tended not to break down until after a crisis. But mostly because there was that small stubborn romantic part of her that wanted to believe Rob had the perfect explanation. He'd calmly exonerate himself with the most plausible reason imaginable, one that she had been too hurt and angry to consider.

She could be a Pollyanna sometimes, but she truly didn't have that much hope. Not really.

She found the marked turnoff and steered the SUV down the uneven road, her heart racing faster than the car. As she got closer to camp, she realized that more tents had been erected, three from what she could see, and two unfamiliar SUVs were parked behind Rob's Sequoia and Seth's truck.

The sight sparked her anger all over again. Had Rob notified everyone in the world?

Everyone but her.

She parked and sat, doing breathing exercises until she was reasonably sure she wouldn't bite his head off before saying hello. From where she sat she couldn't see any activity, but of course her view of the grid area was obstructed.

Just as well, watching them work would probably depress her. Only ten days ago she'd considered herself part of the team. Not going there. She went back to forced deep breathing.

When she finally trusted herself enough to get out of the car, she opened the door and stepped out. Before she could even pocket her keys she saw Jessica and Heather coming out of the supply tent. They stopped when they saw her, and shaded their eyes against the late-morning sun.

Jessica appeared to recognize Karrie first, her face breaking out in an endearing grin, and then both women rushed toward her.

"Karrie!" Jessica nearly knocked her over. She hugged Karrie fiercely. "I'm so glad you're back."

She finally let her go, and to her utter amazement, even Heather hugged her. "This is very cool," the blonde said with a sincere smile. "We were just talking last night how it wasn't right you weren't here for all this excitement."

Karrie bit her lower lip. Of all the blasted things that

almost undid her… She swallowed around the lump in her throat and stepped back. Deep breath. "I can't believe how much has happened in ten days."

"I know." Jessica pushed her sunglasses up, her eyes sparkling. "If I had to describe everything in writing I don't think I could." She smiled wryly. "I tried continuing your journal for you, but I haven't done a very good job."

"Oh, Jessica, that's so nice."

She shrugged. "I'll get your bags for you. Go see Dr. Philips."

Karrie stopped her when she started for the back of the SUV. "I'm not staying."

"What do you mean?"

"Why?" Both women spoke at the same time, staring at her in disbelief.

"I only came to talk with Rob—Dr. Philips. I have to go back to New York tonight."

"Is something wrong?" Jessica's expression fell and she glanced nervously at Heather.

Karrie smiled, tried to keep her tone light. "This isn't my only job, you know. I have a mountain of paperwork on my desk that I haven't tackled since the last trip."

Jessica looked so relieved that Karrie felt a little guilty. Although why disillusion her? The problem would probably work itself out before the students found out what a creep their teacher was.

Bad. Bad. Bad.

She couldn't talk to him. Not like this. She should

have stayed in Las Vegas for the night. Cooled down more before she faced him. Except it wasn't so much about anger, and hurt didn't subside as quickly.

"I can't believe you aren't staying at least one night," Heather said, as they all started to walk toward camp.

"Who do these other cars belong to?" Karrie asked quickly to deflect Heather's new attitude.

"Another team from the University." Jessica rolled her eyes and then brought her sunglasses down into place.

Heather sneered. "Pisses me off. They show up like the friggin' experts after we do all the legwork."

"Not so loud, Heather," Jessica said as they neared the supply tent.

"I don't care if they hear me." She tossed her blond ponytail, and then pointed. "There's one of those know-nothings now."

Karrie hid a smile. Her first genuine one all day. At least some things hadn't changed. Heather was really something else.

"He's talking to Dr. Philips," Heather muttered with disdain as she headed toward the first quad.

Karrie immediately looked in the direction Heather had indicated. There he was, looking tan and healthy and virile. Especially for a rat.

Almost as if he sensed her watching him, he turned suddenly. She was still too far away to gauge his expression. But he had to be surprised. Certainly not pleased. Tough. She hoped he was squirming about now.

He broke away from the other man and started walking toward her.

"He's missed you," Jessica whispered.

Karrie stiffened.

"He's been a real grouch ever since you left. Stays in his tent by himself in the evenings."

Karrie forced a smile.

"Well, I've got lunch duty. I have to get started," Jessica said. "You'll stay for the rest of the afternoon, right?"

"Sure." Karrie smiled. Not sure at all. In fact, she'd probably get the hell out of here as soon as possible.

She waited for him in the shade, unwilling to meet him halfway. The closer he got the more her insides quivered as if she were the one who'd been deceitful.

"I didn't expect you," he said, smiling as he approached, as if nothing were wrong.

For a wild second she thought he was going to kiss her but he stopped a foot away. She didn't return the smile. "Didn't you?"

His expression tightened and he sighed. "Let's go talk."

"That's why I'm here."

"Yeah." He glanced around. Presumably for a private corner.

Jessica stood at the table under the canopy getting out sandwich fixings, and darting worried looks at them. Seth and Todd were digging at the far end of the grid. Two others Karrie didn't recognize crouched at quad four.

"Maybe we should drive to the river," Rob suggested, studying her through his dark glasses.

That hurt. "No."

"I only meant that it would be private. And cooler."

"I don't have a lot of time."

He frowned. "Okay," he said slowly, his voice flat. "How about my tent?"

"My car is still cool. We can sit in there with the air on." Without waiting for a response, she turned and headed back toward the rental.

He followed, and they both climbed in at the same time. She closed her door and turned the key to start the air conditioner. And then turned to him. "You bastard."

"Karrie…"

"Dirty, rotten, conniving bastard. I can't believe I—" She faced forward and hit the steering wheel with the heel of her hand.

"This isn't constructive," he said quietly.

"Screw you."

"I don't blame you for being angry."

"I'm so relieved."

He paused, letting the silence stretch for a few taut moments. "I can explain."

"This ought to be good."

"Karrie…" He reached over to touch her arm, and she jerked away. "Are you calm enough to listen?"

She glared at him. "Now you're concerned about me?"

He pulled off his sunglasses and rubbed his eyes.

Passed a hand over his face. Covered his mouth for a moment, exhaling into his palm. He finally lowered his hand, and her only consolation was that he looked tired.

Maybe he'd tossed and turned a few nights, worrying. She hoped so. It served him right.

"Look, I didn't want to put you in the middle."

She squinted at him. "Where the hell do you think I ended up after getting that letter?"

His eyebrows drew together and uncertainty flickered in his eyes. "From the State?"

"Don't pretend you don't know."

"I knew they'd contact you. I didn't expect it would be this soon."

She shook her head, the fight beginning to drain from her. Leaving the pain behind, taking root so deep in her gut that she wanted to scream. "Why didn't you tell me first? Forget our personal relationship. I went to bat for you. Didn't I deserve that small courtesy of being contacted before you called the State?"

"I didn't call them. They came to me."

"What?"

He nodded. "Guess we did too good a job of convincing that reporter that we had something here."

She gasped. "You didn't contact the State?"

"No."

She put a hand to her mouth. How could she be so stupid? The first article had run last week. "Oh, God, I thought—" She tried to clear her mind. "What did you tell them?"

"The truth."

She took her time, unwilling to leap to another false conclusion. "Which is?"

"Are you asking me if I could have squashed it? Told them the report was premature?"

She said nothing. Just waited.

"Maybe." Regret flashed in his eyes. Or perhaps that's what she wanted to see. "Obviously I didn't."

Okay, so she was partly responsible for this fiasco. Ironically, that made her feel better. Even though he still could have helped her out had he chosen…

"How much heat did you get from Sanax?" he asked softly.

She closed her eyes and laid her head back. "I'm here, aren't I?"

"You were exiled?"

Trying not to smile, she opened her eyes and looked at him. "You think this is a joke?"

"No." He sighed, his expression grim. "I'm sorry. I can't tell you how much."

He did seem contrite. But he had to have known this would happen after volunteering all that information to the reporter. Of course she too should have realized they were toying with Pandora's Box.

God, she had so much to think about. Not the least of which was where all this misunderstanding left them. She still took issue with the fact that he hadn't made an effort to warn her.

"I got reamed a new one," she said. "My boss doesn't

like surprises. I don't, either," she added pointedly. "But I think I've fixed things with him."

"How?"

"By pushing the publicity angle. I truly feel the land would be most valuable to Sanax if it were donated to the University."

His jaw tightened and he stared out toward the site. The pulse on the side of his neck beat erratically. How could he have a problem with that?

"I thought you'd be pleased." She snorted. "Not that my recommendation had anything to do with you. It was based solely on what I feel is in Sanax's best interests."

"Of course," he said absently. "I understand." He looked at her, his gaze searching. "It's complicated. There's more to this."

"What?"

He rolled his shoulders, and stretched his neck to the side.

"You're stalling."

"I know." He briefly closed his eyes and exhaled loudly.

Damn him, he was getting her all worked up. She wiped her clammy palms on her jeans. "Great. Look."

He followed the direction of her gaze. Seth was headed toward them and gesturing frantically.

She let down the window just as he ran up to them. "Dr. Philips, you gotta come see this. Hey, Karrie," he said and ran back toward the site.

"Stay here. I'll be right back." Rob was out of the car in a second.

Like hell. She got out right behind him but he'd already sprinted a good five yards ahead of her. Everyone else already had gathered around what looked to be the third quad. Jessica had an arm wrapped around Heather, who'd stuck a knuckle in her mouth, her gaze glued to something on the ground.

Familiar excitement rushed through her veins as she ran to join them. She'd really missed this. The thrill of discovery. The camaraderie. Expectations. Even the disappointments. Every day was like one big roller-coaster ride. Even after your tenth trip, the dips and curves and loops continued to surprise and excite you.

Everyone was eerily quiet by the time she got there. A man she didn't recognize, long hair, mid-thirties, was crouched with something in his hand. He used a small artist's brush, the kind she'd seen Rob use, as he exposed what appeared to be a pottery shard.

He looked up at Rob and grinned. "What do you think, Dr. Philips?"

Rob stared as if totally transfixed.

Karrie was dying to ask what significance the piece held. Something big obviously. She glanced at Jessica, hoping to catch her eye.

That's when she saw it. Near Seth's feet. She squinted for a better look, and then stooped lower to the ground, and grabbed a handful of soil and sand. She let the bluish-gray dirt slip through her fingers in disbelief.

This couldn't be…

Her heart slammed against her chest. She looked up and met Rob's troubled eyes. He'd known about the silver all along. She didn't know how she knew, but she knew.

Slowly, she straightened, feeling horribly light-headed all of a sudden. She had to get out of here. Back to the car. Back to New York.

No one paid attention to her. Except Jessica. Avoiding the younger woman's eyes, she turned and headed toward her car. Not as quickly as she'd like. Her legs were too shaky.

"Karrie." Rob was beside her suddenly, touching her arm.

She jerked away and walked faster.

"I was about to tell you," he said, staying abreast of her. "I told you it was more complicated."

She stopped and stared him in the eyes. "You knew before I left, didn't you? That's why you kept me away from the site. Me being from around the area, you guessed I might know what that bluish dirt could mean."

His silence spoke volumes.

Muttering a succinct curse, she started toward the car again.

"Wait." He caught up, but wisely didn't touch her. "*Could mean* are the operative words. We both knew the chance of there being a lucrative silver vein under this land is slim to none."

"That isn't the point, Rob. You didn't trust me enough to tell me."

"You, I trust. Sanax wouldn't understand. They'd want the land dug up and evaluated and—"

"And you wouldn't be getting the kudos you're getting."

"It's not about recognition," he said tightly. "You know this is personal."

"Right. I guess I'm disposable."

The pain that creased his face gave her pause. "I made that promise to Joe Tonopah long before I saw you again. I didn't want this to happen. Honey, I thought I could keep you out of it—"

"Don't you dare call me honey." She shook her head, fearful tears would start spilling out. "If you had told me, trusted me, don't you know I would have gone to Sanax and fought for you to have the land?"

"You would have fought, and you would've lost." He stepped closer, his eyes pleading. "And I'm not talking about the land. Your reputation and principles and loyalty would have been challenged."

"Even if there's silver here, I would have made them understand."

"Not a chance." He gave her a patronizing look that made her see red.

"Do you know how used I feel?"

He flinched. "No. Don't—"

She had to get away from him. She'd already made a big enough fool of herself.

"Don't walk away from this, Karrie. We have something—this was our second chance."

"We have nothing," she whispered and ran to the car.

17

KARRIE PUSHED ASIDE her mug of coffee. She was so damn jumpy she couldn't afford another sip of caffeine before her meeting in ten minutes. Exhausted from yesterday's long flight back from Vegas and from too little sleep last night, she'd tried to compensate by overdosing on a strong Jamaican brew from the corner Beanery. Big mistake. Her nerves were stretched tighter than her Aunt Mabel's girdle.

Damn Rob.

The thought slid in before she could put the brakes on it. She couldn't afford to think about him for a fraction of a second. Not that he was worth thinking about.

Damn him.

Sighing with disgust, she glanced at her watch. Nine-fifty-four. Six more minutes. No sweat. She was prepared. Had checked all her facts twice. She was about to prove how wrong Dr. Philips could be. As if she gave a damn about what he thought or did.

Her phone rang. She glanced at her watch again. She had to answer.

She picked up the receiver. "Karrie Albright."

"Karrie? It's Jessica."

"Jessica! Is anything wrong?" Her frantic thoughts immediately went to Rob.

"Oh, no. Nothing."

The relief that descended made her angry. She didn't care about him. Why should she? "Where are you?"

"Laughlin. I'm here only to call you. You left so quickly yesterday."

Karrie sighed and stared at the file folder sitting in front of her. The UNLV-Dr. Philips's file. A month ago she thought she'd never set foot in Nevada again. "Yeah."

"Do you know about Joe Tonopah?"

"Yes, I do."

Jessica paused. "Did you know he's dying?"

Karrie bristled. "Look, Jessica, I'm sure you mean well, but trying to pull sympathy strings isn't helpful."

"All I'm trying to do is put things in perspective."

"Except you can't do that when you don't know all the facts. I appreciate your call. Really, I do. But I have a meeting."

"Get off it, Karrie. I lied to everyone about why I had to come to Laughlin, and then drove for two and a half hours because I got lost, and maybe I don't have all the facts but I like you and I like Dr. Philips, and the least you can do is listen."

Karrie blinked. "Okay."

"This whole dig is about granting a dying man's wish. For Dr. Philips, anyway. Anything we find here won't be a big deal for him as far as his career goes."

She sniffed, and added softly, "Joe came to the site yesterday after you left. A nurse brought him. I wish you could've seen him. He was like—I wish you'd been here. You'd understand why Dr. Philips did whatever he had to do."

Karrie didn't know what to say. She didn't want to sound callous. Nor did she want to hear any of this.

"I want to say one more thing before I hang up," Jessica said. "Cut him some slack, Karrie. Dr. Philips is grieving. He's about to lose a friend and he's already gone into mourning."

"Karrie?" Susan, Sandhill's PA, stuck her head in. "Everyone's waiting."

Karrie nodded. "Look, I really gotta go, Jessica."

"That's okay. I said what I wanted to say." She sighed. "Now I've gotta find my way back."

"Ask for directions, okay?" Karrie cradled the phone between her ear and shoulder as she gathered her notes. "Don't be a guy."

Jessica chuckled. "Think about what I said, okay?"

"Promise." She hung up. Yeah, as if she could think about anything else.

SANDHILL HAD CALLED IN reinforcements. Karrie faced him and Marvin Sandler from Legal. Sitting to her left was Lawrence Dixon, vice president and controller, and next to him was Connie Scalia, one of the Sanax's newest attorneys.

"I've already briefed everyone on your proposal, Ms.

Albright. So let's cut to the chase. What did you find out about this Indian burial ground situation?"

The dismissive way he waved his hand, as if dead Indians were merely a nuisance really annoyed her. Maybe that wasn't what he meant. Or maybe it was. A New Yorker born and bred. What did he know about Native American customs or sacred land?

Now who was being myopic? She mentally chided herself and forced her attention on the strategy she'd devised and practiced until midnight. She needed only to be succinct and confident. Look and sound as if she knew exactly what she was talking about. God help her.

She glanced at her notes, even though she knew precisely what she was going to say. "Frankly, my proposal says it all. The land has never been used. It's too far from any significant power sources to be developed."

"Las Vegas is currently one of the fastest growing cities in the nation," Marvin Sandler said, looking at her over his preppy horn-rimmed glasses. "Surely that must have some impact."

She shook her head, having expected that concern to be voiced. "There's been no growth in that direction, and nothing planned." She passed out copies of statistics she'd gathered about future development in the extended area, including calculations on the projected tax savings a donation would bring.

"You've been out there, I understand." Lawrence Dixon didn't look up from the figures before him. "Is it just desert? That's it. Nothing else?"

"Just desert. Cactus, mesquite, boulders. Snakes."
She shuddered and everyone laughed.

Mr. Dixon frowned thoughtfully. "I guess basically, casino business is the State's main revenue."

"We go to Vegas at least twice a year," Connie Scalia said, and then added almost apologetically, "My husband likes it there. Their motto is The Silver State. But I'm assuming all the silver has been depleted at this point."

All eyes turned to Karrie. She immediately looked at her notes, praying for composure. "Essentially that's true. There are a few mining companies left who control silver producing veins. Occasionally, people mine recreationally, but actually finding a rich vein just doesn't happen anymore."

Two of the men straightened with a fascinated interest that made her briefly falter. She cleared her throat. "It's not even unusual to find bluish-gray dirt at times, indicative of perhaps a small vein, but it's generally not enough to interest anyone but a hobbyist."

Oh, God, she didn't want to do this...

She had no choice. Her conscience ruled. "In fact, I saw some of this bluish dirt myself. It was kind of interesting, really, because—"

"At the site." Sandhill, who'd been remarkably quiet until now, stared at her. "On our land?"

"Yes, but—"

"When?" Dixon and Scalia asked together.

"Yesterday, but—"

"Ms. Albright." Sandhill's sharpness quieted everyone. "You didn't think it important to advise me of this development immediately?"

"Actually, no. Have you ever heard of fool's gold? This is the equivalent. Time and money have been spent chasing such unfruitful dreams."

He held her gaze steady. "You're saying it's impossible for there to be silver in that ground."

She swallowed. "No. Obviously I can't say that."

Everyone began murmuring. Another minute and she'd totally lose control of the situation. Sandhill's angry gaze stayed on her. Or maybe she already had lost.

"We're not a mining company," she said. "I can't see the cost would be justified. On the other hand, donating the land and supporting the search for the burial ground would pay off immeasurably in terms of publicity."

"Thank you, Ms. Albright. We've heard enough." Sandhill sent her a deliberate look that said he wasn't through with her yet. "You can go."

"But we can't disturb the burial ground..." she said, but no one heard. They were all too busy talking excitedly among themselves.

She felt sick to her stomach. But there was nothing left to do or say. Who would have guessed silver fever could strike a bunch of sophisticated Manhattan business people?

Not her.

But Rob had.

Screw him. This was all his fault. But it was over. She never had to see him again.

Swallowing hard, she gathered her notes. When she slipped out the door no one even spared her a glance.

OVER A WEEK OF LAUNDRY had piled up. Something Karrie tried to avoid since she had to schlep the huge bag all the way down to the basement laundry room.

She didn't care. Let it pile up. As long as her supply of chocolate ice cream didn't run out, she'd be just fine. Super. Perfect. Couldn't be better.

She cinched the sash of her kimono, and then looked down at the tie at her waist. Was it her imagination or was the sash getting shorter? For goodness' sakes, she'd only been bingeing on Oreos and ice cream for a week. Just since the meeting with Sandhill and his posse.

Oh, man, that would really do it. She'd never had to worry about her weight before. Of course she was pushing thirty. Damn Rob. That was his fault, too. Somehow. It had to be. Her life was perfect before she'd seen him again.

Well, almost perfect. So what if Madison had been her only date in seven months.

Sighing, Karrie went to the refrigerator, opened the door and stared at the contents. Lots of take-out boxes of leftovers. She should be able to scrape something decent together without getting dressed and going out.

She pulled out a couple of white boxes, opened them and sniffed. Then again, maybe she wasn't all that hungry. She stuffed them back in the fridge, promising herself to put them down the garbage chute the next time she got dressed. Which wouldn't be until Monday if she could help it. And only because, miraculously, she still had a job to go to.

She resumed her position on the couch, swung her feet up onto the coffee table and stared at her bare legs. Unshaven and prickly but lightly tanned. Maybe she should start going to a tanning salon to maintain the color.

Damn Rob.

Why did everything in the world have to remind her of *him?* As soon as she had the energy, she was going to get online and write to the Eve's Apple gang and warn them. This whole Man To Do thing was a big mistake. Huge. Maybe she could save others the grief and disappointment.

Rob may have been right about Sanax's reaction, but he'd still deceived her. That hadn't changed. His good intentions didn't change anything, either.

She thought about what might have happened if she'd never seen the bluish dirt. The land would have been donated to the University and the excavation would have been completed. Evidence of silver probably wouldn't have registered. But if it had, it would have been her butt in a sling. That was it. She knew Rob hadn't wanted to put her in the middle, but that decision should have been hers to make.

Good thing she couldn't reach Jessica. She'd thought about calling a couple of times. Just to see how things were going. And to ask about Joe Tonopah. But it was too soon. Karrie was still too raw.

She closed her eyes for a moment, resting her head on the back of the couch and wishing that Madison wasn't out of town. Then the front door buzzer rang, startling her to her feet. She hadn't ordered pizza or Chinese. Who the hell could it be at eight on a Saturday night?

She depressed the button.

"Ms. Albright?" It was Jimmy, the evening doorman. "You have a visitor. Rob Philips."

Was this a joke? She liked Jimmy. Always tipped him well at Christmas, but sometimes he had a prankster streak in him that...

"Ms. Albright, is it all right to let him up?"

She glanced around her messy apartment. Usually it was perfect. Everything in place. "Yeah, okay."

She didn't have time to think much less pull herself together. So what? What did she care what she looked like? What he thought? She didn't. Period.

That didn't stop her from rushing to the mirror to check her hair and teeth. Her puffy eyes were hopeless. Maybe she shouldn't have let him come up. Met him at the corner coffee shop.

Too late. She heard the knock.

She checked the front of her kimono, made sure she was decent before she opened the door.

He looked like hell. He gave her a small smile. "Thanks for letting me come up."

She folded her arms across her chest. "What do you want?"

His gaze briefly drew to her breasts where they mounded at the flap. "Can I come in?"

"Why? I don't see that we have anything to say to each other."

"Karrie."

"All right." Her bravado slipped. Giving him her back, she led him into the disaster she called her apartment. It was small and cramped, the best she could afford that came with a doorman, and she had to shove aside two self-help books in order to give him room to sit on the couch.

Unfortunately, there was no other chair. No room. But at least she didn't have the bathtub in her kitchen like one of her friends.

"I'm sorry, Karrie," he said simply.

"I'm sure."

He held her gaze. Wouldn't look away. "I was wrong."

"Yes, you were."

He half smiled at that. "I never meant to deceive you but I was caught up in my own guilt and too self-absorbed to see what I was doing. I realize it's no excuse."

"Right again."

"I honestly thought I could protect you by keeping you in the dark."

"You were doing fine up until then." She sighed. "First of all, I'm a grown woman. I don't need anyone to make my decisions for me. I can screw up on my own. Thank you very much."

He didn't smile, didn't speak, only stared expectantly, giving her all the power and control.

"And from now on, you will discuss everything with me that has anything to do with me. Got it?"

His shoulders went back and she saw his Adam's apple move. He looked a little shaken. She knew. She felt shaky herself. It wasn't until the words were out of her mouth that she realized she'd forgiven him.

Slowly, his mouth started to curve. "Can I kiss you now?"

"I haven't brushed my teeth since this morning," she muttered. "You should have called first. What are you doing here anyway?"

He smiled and moved closer. "Unfortunately, I have to go back Tuesday."

She snorted. "We might be on the same flight."

"What?"

"I've been assigned to the Vegas office for a while. Gotta clean up the publicity mess Sanax is about to make out there."

He touched her thigh, and she painfully remembered she hadn't shaved for two days.

"I heard they're fighting the State."

"You'll have to stop digging."

"I know."

"I'm sorry."

"Me, too." He shrugged and slid an arm around her shoulder. "But at least Joe's mind has been put at ease."

"But it'll be in the newspaper. If Sanax starts mining he'll know the land will be disturbed."

"Frankly, I don't think it will come to that. But even

so, he doesn't need to know. He can't read. I'll make sure no one tells him."

She smiled. He was still trying to protect people. They were going to have to have a really good understanding.

He pulled her close and kissed the tip of her nose, and then briefly her lips. "You feel good," he murmured.

"So do you." She snuggled against him. She'd worry about her teeth and legs later.

"Where are you staying in Vegas?" he asked.

"I don't know yet."

After an unexpected silence, she pulled back to look at him. He was staring at her pile of laundry.

"You know," he said. "You could always stay with me. I even have my own washer and dryer."

She laughed until he kissed her breathless.

Epilogue

Two years later

ROB FINISHED DRIVING the tent stakes into the ground while Karrie made them lunch. The damn Wyoming dirt was packed so hard it had taken him a good half hour longer than it should have to get the tent set up.

"Some honeymoon," Karrie grumbled. "You forgot the wine."

"No, I didn't. Two bottles. Your favorite Chardonnay. In the back, on the floor."

She grinned at him. "Are you out of breath?"

Rob grunted. "This isn't sand, you know."

She laughed and sauntered up to him with a taunting sway of her hips. "Must be getting old," she said poking him in the ribs. "And soft."

"Oh, yeah?"

She screamed when he scooped her up in his arms. But no one would hear. Not a soul around for a hundred miles. Just the way he liked it. They both did. She'd gotten very used to the outdoors in the past year.

In fact, since she'd transferred to Sanax's Las Vegas

branch almost two years ago, they'd gone on almost every dig together, and had taken advantage of every three-day weekend to go camping and kayaking. He'd worried at first that she'd miss the excitement of city life, that she'd resent turning down a promotion to be with him. Instead, she moaned and groaned every time she had to go back to New York for a meeting, complaining about the noise and traffic, and whining that she had to wear pantyhose again.

Rob smiled as he found a carpet of pine needles and laid her down. God, he didn't think he'd ever get enough of her. Whenever she had to leave a dig early to get back to the Vegas office, he was restless and plagued with insomnia until he joined her there. Funny, how he didn't mind being in the classroom so much anymore. Not when he had her to look forward to every evening.

She wasted no time in unbuttoning his flannel shirt and running her palms up his chest. It took him a second to yank off her sweatshirt. Braless, she was left bare.

"Kind of nippy, isn't it?" she said with a slight shiver.

"I'll warm you up."

"I bet."

He covered her body with his, reveling in the feel of her smooth soft skin pressed to his chest. And knew, he had to be the luckiest man in the world.

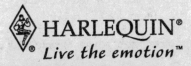

If you enjoyed what you just read,
then we've got an offer you can't resist!

Take 2 bestselling
love stories FREE!
Plus get a FREE surprise gift!

Clip this page and mail it to Harlequin Reader Service®

IN U.S.A.
3010 Walden Ave.
P.O. Box 1867
Buffalo, N.Y. 14240-1867

IN CANADA
P.O. Box 609
Fort Erie, Ontario
L2A 5X3

YES! Please send me 2 free Blaze™ novels and my free surprise gift. After receiving them, if I don't wish to receive anymore, I can return the shipping statement marked cancel. If I don't cancel, I will receive 4 brand-new novels each month, before they're available in stores! In the U.S.A., bill me at the bargain price of $3.99 plus 25¢ shipping and handling per book and applicable sales tax, if any*. In Canada, bill me at the bargain price of $4.47 plus 25¢ shipping and handling per book and applicable taxes**. That's the complete price and a savings of at least 10% off the cover prices—what a great deal! I understand that accepting the 2 free books and gift places me under no obligation ever to buy any books. I can always return a shipment and cancel at any time. Even if I never buy another book from Harlequin, the 2 free books and gift are mine to keep forever.

150 HDN DZ9K
350 HDN DZ9L

Name	(PLEASE PRINT)	
Address	Apt.#	
City	State/Prov.	Zip/Postal Code

Not valid to current Harlequin Blaze™ subscribers.

Want to try two free books from another series?
Call 1-800-873-8635 or visit www.morefreebooks.com.

* Terms and prices subject to change without notice. Sales tax applicable in N.Y.
** Canadian residents will be charged applicable provincial taxes and GST.
All orders subject to approval. Offer limited to one per household.
® and ™ are registered trademarks owned and used by the trademark owner and or its licensee.

BLZ04R   ©2004 Harlequin Enterprises Limited.